THE INVERTED CITY

THE INVERTED CITY

KARAN ANAND SHANDILYA

PARTRIDGE

Copyright © 2016 by Karan Anand Shandilya.

ISBN:	Hardcover	978-1-4828-7244-6
	Softcover	978-1-4828-7243-9
	eBook	978-1-4828-7242-2

Print information available on the last page.

To order additional copies of this book, contact
Partridge India
000 800 10062 62
orders.india@partridgepublishing.com

www.partridgepublishing.com/india

Contents

Acknowledgement

To my dearest parents,
When all mist will fade,
When all the lights are dim,
I shall dwell still in dream,
Thank you for letting me tread in clouds...

1

The Rude Voice

'Conscience has plagued your mind. The illusions of the world have warped your reality, my friend. There is but one way out . . .'

Aryan woke with a start. His brow was covered in sweat, yet his heart was calm. A cold wind howled beyond the moisture-laden windowpanes, making them tremble delicately. The ruffle of dry leaves gave the illusion of autumn, an autumn gone cold.

In the meandering winds, prophecies were being whispered; all was about to change.

The sound of water dripping out of an unfixed pipe tore through the shrieks of the howling wind like a diamond blade. Aryan had been experiencing a multitude of vivid dreams lately which mostly consisted of a certain voice unceremoniously and constantly antagonizing him. His appreciation towards these vivid portrayals of a multitude of delirious outbursts had dwindled lately. The voice considered him incapable of most human expression and had even gone to the extent of claiming him to have the sublime privilege of being the rabbit that got lost.

This would seem rather vague, but in the defence of the voice in Aryan's head, most rabbits don't really proclaim the ambitions of having much of a journey, so to get lost on a path that does not exist is quite embarrassing. The exact words were 'There is no journey, nor is there a path, yet here you hop along, the rabbit that got lost'.

Aryan meandered through countless such dreams, but the most recent one truly frightened him. The reasons were unclear, but he was afraid nonetheless.

'You petty fool! Oh, you miserly fool, you dread my distaste, and yet you pine for my voice.'

The voice in Aryan's head interrupting even his general thoughts had become quite a common occurrence, one which did not go down too well in his mind. However, what frightened Aryan was the fact that this voice came from his own conscience, so what if his mind considered him an insignificant afterthought in his own dream and now regular reality?

To witness one's own mind rebel against itself is not a pleasurable occurrence, but what is worse than the scenario described would probably be the uncertainty of not knowing whether the voice truly belonged to your mind.

To this voice, Aryan would, on most occasions, reply on such a note: 'Must you interrupt my thoughts even while I am awake? Let me lament of your dreary and incoherent babble in peace. Leave my reality alone.'

Aryan was certain someone was trying to rip through the physical details of his conscience and flow into his improbable yet conceivable reality. Such a thought would diminish the moral of any individual, but to him, it was comforting. He did not feel alone. Friend or foe, Aryan knew for certain there was someone waiting for him in a dimension he was yet to discover. On the few occasions when he was lounging in a chair or sipping on coffee, he would think of the probabilities of facing the realities of a parallel truth, and it would create a sense of tension in his already morphed mind. But then again, that was the extent to which he thought of this scenario, which is quite an anticlimax to the numerous occasions he had been antagonized by the voice.

Still in bed, Aryan gathered his meandering thoughts which, from dreaming of the possibilities of parallel realities, had drifted to the metaphysics of the proper noun and devious-looking birds he had encountered in his varied travels, most exotic and almost all fictitious to the common man living in the ordinary dimension.

2

The Room

As his gaze caressed the environment, Aryan knew it was his room for certain yet different. The bed he lay on was in the exact same spot as moments earlier when he was contemplating various vague probabilities, but the upholstery had changed for certain—this there was no denying, yet not very surprising.

There was nothing spectacular in a random change of upholstery. On the contrary, Aryan considered it to be quite delinquent an event to not have upholstery changing without notice, varying shades of white and most without stains, just the way he liked it.

This mattress, however, wasn't without stains and not particularly white.

Aryan generally never embarked on the rather adventurous task of sleeping on this mattress.

'Mattresses aren't meant to be slept upon. They seem too unnatural and spongy to be able to support one's dreams.'

The last time he had dared to sleep on his mattress was due to the fact that the voice in his head told him not to. The voice said, 'To witness the unravelling of the universe, you must feel the cold surface your feet tread on. You must not let your dreams be absorbed by the unnatural white. Let the stone be their witness.'

Aryan did not want to witness the unravelling of the universe, nor did he want the stones to witness his dreams, whatever that meant, and chose to sleep on the unnatural white.

At this moment, he lay on his mattress because he had decided that the unnatural white was quite comfortable on certain occasions—this he could not deny.

It often gave him the illusion of sleeping on a carcass. It disjointed him from the universe, made him feel alone. The spongy mattress seemed to absorb all his thoughts, emotional echoes. It disjointed him from everything apart from the voice. The voice never ceased. It went on relentlessly, constantly speaking to Aryan and, on more than one occasion, not being particularly friendly either. This did not, however, get Aryan to get rid of the mattress. It was a need, not a place to dwell.

As the wolves in the wind howled away the sorrows of the night, the thought of the spongy disconnect from the universe slowly dwindled away into an obscure corner of his mind.

Dawn had arrived, and through some crevice not visible to him, a narrow ray of orange light penetrated through his obscure thoughts, causing him to look around and, to a certain extent, realize his bearings. Aryan had begun to experience a prevailing sense of change. The colour of the wall adjacent to his bed had changed and not for the first time. It was a deep red, a kind of red that would endure even through the darkest nights.

The symbolic significance of these changes in colours seemed an unconceivable notion to Aryan, but he was certain it wasn't caused by the voice.

He would have been aware, for the voice did not leave things to chance and, on the contrary, would often boast of upcoming misdemeanours that were to pester Aryan. The voice at least had the courtesy of not leaving him in the dark, which gave Aryan the ability to tolerate and sometimes even enjoy these obscene and unnecessary profanities.

He didn't mind the occasional change in scenario and, hence, did not ponder too much into this occurrence. Aryan had long grown used to the changes in his physical environment. He, as you can imagine, had not the slightest inclination to who was responsible for these acts.

It barely pressed on his conscience, and neither did it matter, for there were far more pressing matters he had to deal with. Fortunately for him, he could not remember them, so he decided to go back to his not-very-white mattress and cut out all thoughts and visions.

'Coffee . . .'

'*Coffee* . . . coffee . . . Uhhh, I need some coffee.'

He did not know how many moments had passed since he had decided to lie back on the mattress, but now there was no orange light penetrating through the crevice; instead, there he was, sitting in the same room with his proximities very well illuminated by daylight. The only concern was he did not know where the light was coming from, for there was no visible source for this majestic orange.

Followed by a forced silence, the voice in his head spoke. 'It matters not for light is light and darkness is a fugitive, such a fickle mind, such a dreary thought.'

Aryan ignored it.

'Thank you for the coffee.'

Aryan had turned his head moments later to find a hot, steaming cup of black coffee waiting for him on his nightstand.

'Just the way you like it.'

With a complete lack of desire to respond, Aryan replied, 'How may I ask is that?'

Aryan clearly had no idea how he liked his coffee or if he really even wanted it, but at the moment, his conscience craved for it quite dearly.

'With a little thought.'

This statement was followed by Aryan's mind echoing with peals of uncontrollable laughter.

This made absolutely no sense to Aryan, who decided to disregard the statement and sip on his coffee.

'I'm glad you did not reply to my statement. It was meant to be rhetoric.'

The laughter was reignited.

Aryan was accustomed to the random outbursts of the voice, and this clearly was not the first time he had witnessed the voice quite heartily enjoying its own comments. Aryan maintained his straight face and continued to sip on his coffee, which had now, for some reason, gone rather cold.

As he gulped done the insipid coffee, Aryan could feel a slight discomfort in his throat. It felt as though the fluid was manoeuvring around something lumpy, preventing the normal route the coffee would have taken to reach his cold belly. He placed his hand gently on the side of his throat, and there he felt a strange mass. He imagined it to make him look like a bulbous frog-like creature. This was the same mass that would appear every time he was having his coffee and very ceremoniously disappear when he was done.

'You're just another toad in a dreamy whirlpool.'

Not very amused after feeling the lumpy mass, Aryan replied rather bitterly, 'Your level of dialogue has rather declined.'

'I am you, and you are me.'

On the side tables, which as expected were not even remotely close to the vicinity of the mattresses, also a major fragment of Aryan's anti-universe, lay a tattered pile of papers. In them he could see words scribbled, but he couldn't read them.

'The reason I chose to call this my anti-universe is due to the fact that for as far as I can remember, it has disconnected me from the existentialism of the parallel dimensions that plague my mind. The soft sponge on this carcass knots my dreams into invisible walls, claiming dominance on my emptiness. I also call it my anti-universe because it sounds rather deep and, I am sure, will appeal to the voice.'

'What a melodramatic outburst, and I always thought of you as the silent one.'

Aryan imagined this unnecessarily condescending tone to be accompanied by a rather-smug smirk.

'Did I say that out aloud? How strange, I could swear I didn't feel my lips moving.'

'Nor did I, but to me, it doesn't matter. I am you, and you are me.'

'Now you repeat your statements too.'

'I do feel you are rather deep, but again, maybe it's just me.'

As another pointless conversation dwindled into opacity, a sound disturbed the silent ambience surrounding Aryan and the voice.

The pile of papers full of ink lying next to him seemed to be making a kind of ruffling sound, yet they showed no movement.

It seemed, to the general observer, as if some imaginary force was going through the contents of the pages deviously, trying not to get noticed, or it could have very easily been the sound of the dry leaves swooshing around the dew-covered windows in the cold winter breeze.

The side table on which the papers rested lay in the centre of the room, or at least the centre of the visible portion of the room.

As Aryan noticed the objects gracing his surroundings, he noticed the peculiarity of the side tables.

'The last time I saw my side tables, they were made of mahogany wood and had the crisp smell of roasted cinnamon. The almond-coloured drawers seemed the perfect place to store parchments of paper, and yet here in the centre of the visible portion of my room, all I see are two stark white boxes with no openings!'

As expected the voice interrupted this flow of thoughts.

'Such a melodic description of a chest. The mahogany was clarity in your obscurity, and now even that has perished. Had I been responsible, I would have enjoyed gloating over your piteous demeanour.'

'Please go away . . .'

Aryan did not mean this; however, the absence of his original side tables had affected him to a much greater extent than his colour-changing walls, the reason being quite a plausible one too.

The contents of a drawer can be quite frightening, especially if they contain words in any form. Now Aryan knew the words scribbled away in the parchments in his mahogany drawers. It had taken him a reasonably long time to grow accustomed to them. Now he would have to readapt to new words, and who knew where they would lead him to. Unfortunately for him, his words no longer inhabited the white side table.

'To empty your thoughts into a side table is too overpowering for the object. No wonder it does not appear like it did earlier. Your mind is empty, and the side table full of throbbing dreams. Stark white it is.'

This time the opinion of the voice did make sense to Aryan.

He realized how overpowering the words must have been for the poor, ignorant side table. He had, without realizing, altered its complete being.

The greatest dilemma now was him not knowing what thoughts he had emptied into the drawers and what they had mingled with.

How were they to alter his perspective? And to know this, there was only one solution. First, he would have some coffee.

Aryan vaguely remembered placing his thoughts in the mahogany side table—clearly a mistake, for now his thoughts had completely morphed them and transformed them into stark-white side tables.

'This is probably because your thoughts are so meagre and ordinary. I pity the fate of the beholders of your dreams.' The voice in his head smirked.

'Rather unnecessary.' A frustrated Aryan blurted out, 'I'm sure they were thoughts I believed in, cherished, and nourished. This drastic change of appearance does not surprise me.'

Aryan felt his strength leave his body. The reverberations of the voice seemed to grow louder and stronger as his already-diminished ego began to falter further. His beliefs had been questioned, the few ideas he based his existence upon.

He felt the urge to scream, for he was certain his beliefs were insignificant and stark. He had not the strength to open the drawers and see what the contents of his stored dreams were.

'It seems to me as though the universe has failed you. Your dreams are misty, and there is silence in your chaos. Your illusions now lie with me, and I am you.'

Aryan looked towards the side tables. He was certain this was where the voice came from. It seemed similar to the voice in his head, yet it was different.

'Do you truly believe I am only in your head? I am everywhere.'

'Maybe the starkness of the side tables isn't due to the lack of thought. It is possible that it has nothing to do with my dreams!'

Aryan sensed strength return to his voice.

'It is, and yet it is not.'

This time, however, Aryan realized the lack of conviction in the reply.

'Blue birds flew across the sea,

Monsters ravaged the mountains,

I saw a serpent once,

Her eyes were blue and her soul dark.'

The voice in Aryan's head now sang these verses steadily as he dozed back into another restless slumber.

This was the first time Aryan had questioned the voice that emanated from within the confines of his dreary world, the first time the voice was timid. Aryan's dreams were silent.

For once, he slept with no voice bellowing through his hollow mind.

Aryan awoke, this time calm and not startled. This was strange to him. The absence of the voice did not bring him the joy he had anticipated, but then again, he didn't really know how that felt or how most emotions felt any more. Aryan was hollow, an empty container with a pestering voice in it.

'Boy, missing me already! After all the complaints and jeers, the mighty container needs his voice back.'

'A coffee would be nice.'

The absence of relief in Aryan's voice did not stop the voice from basking in its glory and ensured Aryan got a nice smouldering cup of coffee.

As always, once Aryan was awake, he looked around to gather his belongings, and not unlike previously, his vision was blurry and covered in a layer of mist. The dream Aryan did not have involved a very familiar face, a face he had not dreamt of in a while.

Aryan, at the moment, could not recall what exactly happened in this vision, which was strange because he did not recall dreaming at all.

This was very vague to him, for only in his illusions did he have a true identity and perspective.

The extremities of the room were covered in shadowy darkness, a darkness into which Aryan had long since stopped bothering to ponder over.

'I suppose my illusions have dissipated into absolute darkness, or maybe I just need to replace the lights.'

Strange voices always emanated from the shadowy corners of his room, silent pitter-patter of feet and a scribbling of pen against paper.

If at all, they were even the ends of the room. Aryan had never ventured beyond the lit portion of his room, for the darkness and chaos of his hollow mind were pressing-enough issues to bother about what lay in the darkness of his current reality.

'This person that you are so delighted to have met again in your dreams, you do not even recall your conversations with, so why this favouritism?'

Aryan smiled. He felt as though for once he had prevailed over the nuisance in his mind.

'Ahh . . . I sense jealousy now, and I thought you had no emotion, just a prevailing sense of annoyance.'

Aryan felt a certain feeling in his mind that made him feel elevated. He was certain he was floating, but he dare not look, might he fall back down.

The voice laughed. 'You won't be floating for too long. It's just your ego. Wait till you get to know him better. He is no one's friend.'

The voice sounded frightened about something, which gave Aryan great joy and caused him to feel the sensation of floating even higher, but still he dared not look down.

'Let me tell you a story about ego . . .'

'No,' Aryan interrupted rather abruptly, revelling in the sensation.

'Focus,' yelped the voice and then went silent.

Aryan realized that this time he had not chosen to sleep on the mattress and, hence, had the strange dream which he still couldn't recall. His mattress was white yet covered with grime. A wise decision to sleep on the floor, thought Aryan, as he realized he wasn't floating either.

'If this mattress was the sole identity of the universe, an immeasurable mass of chaos, a distant disconnect that plagues your mind, it has every right to be covered in grime.'

The voice was back and was with great gusto backing up the dirty mattress.

'The mattress is the universe, tainted with human thoughts.'

'Tainted with my thoughts?' asked Aryan excitedly.

'You are no longer the universe, and yet the universe dwells within your reach.'

The voice in his head sounded bored. It didn't like answering questions.

'You have failed the universe.'

This was unnecessary, for he hadn't done anything to be accused of such a heinous act.

'At least my thoughts are plaguing something pure!'

'A spark in his eye . . . Well, well, so he does have emotion.'

Everything faded out very rapidly, and Aryan's vision was cloaked with a blanket of darkness as he fell back into a slumber.

Aryan awoke this time, seated upright on a chair which seemed to have come straight out Siegfried Bing's Maison de l'Art Nouveau.

The chair had delicately curving lines with animal motifs which was a little strange.

The characteristic floral motifs did not seem to find any relevance on this chair and had probably been devoured by the rabbit motifs.

Curving vines graced the back of the hardwood chair, and a single sparrow flew across the corner of the graciously outward curve of the back of the beautiful chair. The cushion had padded on it Victorian upholstery, mohair to be precise. It was a shade of deep velvet, and the fabric tufted. It seemed out of place yet blended right in.

Aryan wasn't very fond of this chair, for he felt it was too grandeur for his liking, a rather bourgeois asset, and to him quite embarrassing.

The sparrow on the chair looked towards Aryan, only his eyes moved.

'Now let's be honest here. None of us really like being a permanent part of antique furniture. I'm a sparrow, I need to fly.'

'Fly to where? You're carved out of wood!'

'Having conversations with a chair now, are we?'

'I never asked for this chair to be here, and if the birds on the chairs have complaints, then maybe the chair needs to go. I have enough problems already to be dealing with the psychology of a carved wooden bird.'

'I'm a sparrow.'

'So am I!'

On hearing this unprecedented and unexpected outburst from Aryan, there was a sudden silence in the room. The sparrow had decided to return to its recluse, silently sulking. The voice, on the other hand, had decided to take its chance with Aryan.

'The boy is arguing with wooden sparrows now!'

He could have sworn he heard a distant disgruntled chirp in the background.

'I really don't like this chair. Nothing else has definition. Then why must I have this elaborate piece of wood with all these unhappy creatures on them?'

'The purpose is majestic, your complaints avoidable.'

3

The Head Administration of the Low-Voltage Industry

Aryan turned the dial on the radio.

His coffee had gone cold yet again. The radio had a black chagrin covering and was assembled in plywood. It was one of those Soviet models created to counter the more expensive radios of the 1935 Soviet era.

The radio had a removable black cover with ventilating holes in it. On the front, there were the controls of the set, with the tuning handle right in the centre. The tuner for the radio was in one of the window slits, with what seemed to be a vertically moving scale.

One of the two knobs on either side was for the volume control; Aryan could never figure out which.

A loud sound blared through the paper diaphragm of the radio, making his presence felt. 'My name is P. A. Lokhvitsky, and I am a radio.'

Aryan looked upon Lokhvitsky with a certain sense of awe; it seemed to him as though he was running on some new-world technology. Energy seemed to emanate from within the confines of the leather box turning everything around him grey. Aryan turned his gaze downwards, and he knew for certain he had lost all colour. Then the radio fell back into silence, just the way it had burst out of silence, without a warning and unhesitatingly.

'When the old sinister moon rises,

Upon hollow dwellings we ponder,

Gazing into the streaming light,

We must promise not to falter.'

The voice in his head slowly mumbled as though into a distance, and for once, Aryan felt his need to be silent, an unavoidable constant.

Something was stirring his conscience; he could sense it. This was different from his dreams. Sounds seemed sharper, and the silence cold, colder than usual at least.

On most occasions, Aryan enjoyed the silence of the terrifying darkness, the absence of dreams, and voices calmed him. He felt in these moments negated.

His fingers were twitching now, and he could sense the strong aroma of coffee. The fragrance slowly trickled through his being as though being pushed forth very gently by an invisible ego. The fragrance generated a memory in his blank mind, one he would have rather avoided.

'The footsteps were following him, the kind of footsteps no one really likes. All around him there was light. A bright sunlight fell upon his brow, illuminating the trickle of sweat running down his face. Moments later, he was looking down upon himself treading along a purple path . . .'

Her voice, the voice from his dream, had returned.

Aryan was breathing very heavily when he lost the vision of his conscious dream. He seemed to have lost most of the already diminished strength in his body, panting slowly and precariously.

The radio came back to life. 'Are your visions trying to diminish your knowledge of my most recent awakening?' The voice in the radio sounded curious. 'As you might have guessed, I am not a voice in the radio. I am the radio itself speaking to you. I am P. A. Lokhvitsky.'

The voice boomed out aloud, tearing through the weak defenceless mind that was Aryan.

'Mr Lokhvitsky, I must admit you have a rather strange voice.'

'Do you find it amusing? Because I share the exact same sentiment towards you.'

'I hope I have not offended you, Mr Lokhvitsky.'

'Offense is an understatement, boy. You are lucky I haven't shot you in the chest, you democratic beast.'

'I apologize for any miscommunication. I really am no democrat though.'

'Silence, you pig, I have a message for you.'

Mr Lokhvitsky's voice vanished from the frequency plaguing the air and was followed by a low whistling sound. How long this sound meandered in Aryan's presence, he couldn't tell, but it was absolutely horrific to his scarred mind. No coffee could mend this gruesome radio babble.

'Listen, the whistle has gone!'

It seemed to Aryan as if the whistle had annoyed the voice in his head as much as it had him.

'That sound can annoy anyone. Do you not think I have emotions! Listen, listen . . .'

There was a crisp crackling sound, the kind of sound dry leaves lying beneath their shedding mother would make upon being tread on by barefoot lovers on a cold autumn morning.

It was magical and tragic. The sound was haunting, and Aryan wished it would go on forever. It was the kind of white noise that could eliminate complete thought from one's mind.

'It truly is magical, isn't it?'

The crackling stopped, and slowly through the darkness, Aryan heard a voice emanating from the radio.

'It cannot be.' Aryan's voice trembled.

'It is . . .'

'Ave verum corpus, natum
de Maria Virgine,
vere passum, immolatum
in cruce pro homine
cuius latus perforatum
fluxit aqua et sanguine:
esto nobis praegustatum
in mortis examine.
O Iesu dulcis, O Iesu pie,
O Iesu, fili Mariae.
Miserere mei. Amen.

And, fellows, your sins . . . the coffee to reignite your soul. The magic man has spoken. Byrd, ladies and gents, cats with hats . . . finally tonight, we celebrate the innocence of our universe. We welcome, you all . . . dress to rise. Your calls will be answered and other such rubbish.'

The radio fell silent. The symphony had brought tears to Aryan's eyes. It brought back memories of days with thought. He could sense this yet not recollect.

'That was Byrd, my dear friend.'

'I know who Byrd is!' said Aryan. He seemed very distracted. There seemed to be a lingering anxiety in his voice.

'It feels like a time infinite. My suffering and angst have been unbearably long.'

'It appears as though you have been awaiting something, Aryan.'

'Not any more, not any more.'

'Who's being dramatic now?'

Aryan did not particularly understand or care for the spirituality of Byrd's words, nor did he even bother contradicting his symbolism. The strength of his voice, however, was enough to create a reverberating calm in the chaos of his being.

'It is the sorrow you rejoice in, my dear friend, and with sorrow comes light.'

The voice seemed calming for once, yet Aryan was too agitated to bother.

'What light could there possibly be with the darkness of sorrow, you fool?'

'The mask on your face has vanished, Aryan. It is this light I talk about. It does not need to illuminate. Some light is better dark.'

'You make no sense,' muttered Aryan, rather distracted by what was going to occur next.

The radio had fallen silent awhile back; Aryan's mind, however, following the calming presence of the white noise, had gone into overdrive.

He was having heated arguments with the voice, and it was diminishing his strength.

There was no coffee either.

'What time is it?'
'You seem rather tired, if I may presume correctly.'
There was a sudden darkness in Aryan's conscience.
'Falling asleep, are we?' sniggered the voice.

4

The Timeless Man

Aryan awoke with a tingling feeling running along his spine, with no direction in particular. It was as though his mind had abandoned its petty duties of running his body in the appropriate manner and was now just fooling around.

Aryan had begun to enjoy this sensation as he stretched out his legs and heard the cracking in his joints. This gave him immense pleasure. The tingling stopped immediately.

'That was rather rude of you. Why can you not let me enjoy a moment of pleasure? This is—'

'My dear comrade, meet me, for tonight we celebrate the innocence of our nonexistent souls. Meet me . . . meet us when the clock . . .' A loud blaring sound interrupted Aryan's meandering complaints about his self-righteous conscience, a sound with the voice of P. A. Lokhvitsky.

This interruption created chaos in his mind yet again. It agitated and excited his being. This was definitely the message he had been awaiting.

'Next time, do try not to interrupt my words with your petty thoughts.'

Aryan looked rather sheepish, a very unlikely occurrence considering the fact that he did not care much for voices and sounds.

'I am—'

'Don't you dare speak to me. Who would have heard of someone trying to talk back to a radio?'

There was a crackling of white noise, and the radio went silent.

'This is definitely it,' muttered Aryan.

'I still don't understand what you're going on about.' The voice in his head sounded confused, not a very common occurrence.

'I think you know exactly what this is all about. Now stay silent while I think about my plan of action.'

'Oh my, a plan of action, maybe a nap,' sniggered the voice.

Aryan ignored the voice and began hunting frantically for a clock.

'There must be a clock somewhere.'

Aryan had lost all track of time, not knowing what time of day or what day it was. It had never really mattered to him, and that is probably why the clock had vanished into obscurity. He had been cooped up like a pigeon in a cage, his thoughts meandering in the vicinity of being repetitive and rather drab.

'That is assuming that the thoughts of pigeons are boring and repetitive,' giggled the voice, very amused with itself, or so it seemed.

'I'm sure pigeons don't really have too many thoughts that would cause the questioning of universal pathos.'

'Is that what you would consider amusing? Seems quite nonsensical to me.'

Aryan stared at what would have been the voice had it had a form with a cold stony glare.

'You know what?' Aryan sounded firm, as though with an agenda to set things straight.

'What?' muttered the voice, not seeming very anticipant of the coming onslaught.

Aryan gazed away from the imaginary form of the voice. His eyes dulled again. 'I've never really seen a pigeon in a cage before.'

Aryan spoke in a slow-pitched voice that made him sound darker than his thought actually was. There was something not very ordinary brewing in the cold darkness of Aryan's vicinity.

As Aryan completed this thought, he felt a flutter of feathers, and as he stretched his arm out, he felt no fingers, just a pair of greyish wings, and not particularly impressive either. It seemed as though he now truly was a pigeon in captivity. The first caged pigeon.

'Coo.' It was a coo of discontent. Aryan clearly did not consider his arms transforming into pigeon wings a pleasurable one. He did not even dare see what had occurred to the rest of his body, maybe a proud pigeon crest; he was hoping he wasn't one of those coloured pigeons. That would be quite embarrassing.

His thoughts had begun to meander away from the clock, and this was disgruntling to Aryan. This was no time to transform into an embarrassingly annoying bird.

At that very moment, out of the silence, there burst out what sounded like an anthem. It was in a strange language, but these were what the words meant.

'God, save the Tsar!

Strong and majestic,

Reign for glory, for our glory!

Reign to foes' fear,

Orthodox Tsar.

God, save the Tsar!'

Aryan sat up in shock, and there it was all along, the clock.

'Why did it have to be the Kremlin?'

'Silence!' a strangely unfamiliar and rather commanding voice boomed.

There was a white noise in the background, and the radio came to life. 'Is that you, Mikhail?'

'Indeed it is. It is I, Mikhail Cheremnykh. And who might it be that mentions my name with such casual ease?'

The radio remained silent, dare he offend the voice emanating so courageously from the clock.

'The tsar forbade my predecessor from chanting the anthem of our fatherland. He always considered us an inferior race to the human kind even though we were always perched high up looking down upon those frivolous clowns. God save the Tsar. God save the Tsar.'

There was a sudden chime of bells. They did intend to sound majestic, but it seemed as though they had been battered and now were just a reminiscence of their once-great chime.

'Ohh, this is going to be sublime,' yelped the radio.

'Mikhail is going to sing us "Internationale"!'

Mikhail's voice purred. He seemed pleased by the adulation.

'I expect you to sing the chorus with me . . .

Stand up, ones who are branded by the curse,

All the world's starving and enslaved!

Our outraged minds are boiling,

Ready to lead us into a deadly fight.

We will destroy this world of violence

Down to the foundations, and then

We will build our new world.

He who was nothing will become everything!'

There was an abrupt pause. It was almost as if he had forgotten the words or didn't seem to know how to carry on.

'Silence . . . silence, boy. Do you not realize I know what you are thinking? Do you not realize I see everything? Remember and do not forget, I am the mighty Mikhail. Do not doubt me again, for consequences you might not wish to assume.'

A silence, a rather long drab, and unnecessary silence followed.

'What a shame, what a pity, and to think we were going to be blessed with the beautiful poetry and the sublime voice of Mr Mikhail. I really did want him to finish. Everything is ruined now.'

There was a loud chiming sound, but the poetry did not ensue.

'The dream has passed,

None left,

Dread and sorrow all have passed,

Yet a sliver of ice in his blood,

Gazing upon his audience of tiny people,

He had risen, yet none were around,

Lonely and faithless,

The chiming clock sang his song,

Not once did he falter, not once did he fade,

He knew now, there is no jinn nor is there a god.

Time to fly, time to go,

Far ahead a crimson son burnt,

The mad hatter floating as she chimed her song,

White clouds and a moisture-laden goodbye,

A bottomless pit of dust and smiles,

All is dry all is lost,

Here comes the rain to wash it all away . . .'

There was a tingling sensation in Aryan's belly. This was a message. He did not understand its significance yet he knew something was amiss.

'Slumber is good for the dormant boy, rise now.'

'Bravo, bravo! Down with those of whom you speak of and up with the other ones.'

The radio was thrilled.

'Is that you, Lokhvitsky, you fool?'

'Yes, it is! Look at you looking as majestic as ever.'

'Quiet, you miser, I have a message for this human with pigeon arms. Who would have thought that I, Mikhail, the mighty Mikhail, would be made a messenger for a fool of these proportions? I expected someone rather majestic.'

Aryan looked quite taken aback. This was just a glancing emotion though, and he was truly waiting with great anticipation for the message. This was the moment of reckoning or at least something that would get him out of this horrific room.

'If you are done with your pondering, we would like to now hear the message.'

Aryan was quite curious to why the radio, or P. A. Lokhvitsky, or whoever he was, wanted to hear the message with so much zest, but in his present state, he couldn't really care.

Following a brief moment of silence, a truly majestic voice emanating from the clock broke the cloak of silence. All the members of the room seemed to be waiting so eagerly.

The voice was royal like a velvet robe. It seemed as though it was almost purring.

'My dear friend and comrade, the time has arrived for you to step into the light. Do so when you feel the moment is truly the moment of your reckoning. Nine o'clock to be precise.'

A slight crackle resonated in the air.

'Nine o'clock really . . . Don't be late.'

The clock went silent.

'That was a great message, Mikhail. You truly are a blessed messenger.'

The eagerness to please Mikhail was uncanny and delightfully obvious in the voice of P. A. Lokhvitsky.

He was, however, greeted only by a silence as Mikhail, the voice from the miniature Kremlin clock, wasn't in any mood to reciprocate this overly obvious adulation towards him.

Aryan stared at his newly acquired appendages and seemed rather amused. He wondered if he could fly around a little. It would seem quite wasteful if the wings did not serve that purpose at the very least.

'*Focus,* boy!' Mikhail yelled rather loudly.

'Oh, Mikhail, you're back!'

'Quiet, Lokhvitsky, I have no patience for your silly words. It is nine o'clock, and the temperature is stubborn. Rise, it is time to fly. The magic man awaits your presence.'

'Bah, why is everyone so dramatic?'

After a long and unprecedented pause, the voice in Aryan's head finally got a word in, the final word as always.

5

The Departure

'All the clocks, and all the chimes,
All the ghosts and all the wine,
All the men and all the swine,
Dreamt of only one, just one time.'

The voice in Aryan's head was restless; he was trying to awaken him with absolutely no success.

'The reason for all the chaos that had ensued prior to this is now a vision of our protagonist of the moment. Aryan curled up like a ball, trembling with fear or maybe indignation or probably because he chose to sleep on an ice-cold floor when he could very easily have been snug under a warm blanket—one will just have to wait and find out.'

Aryan frowned. He was trying to avoid the voice, but with no success.

'Did you just narrate my current state to an invisible audience?'

Aryan gasped. He wasn't bemused. He felt violated.

'You left me no choice. It was either that or me hanging around doing nothing of great consequence really.'

'Ahhh . . . I cannot do this any more, and also that poem about the man and his swine was horrific.'

With a momentous gasp, Aryan was on his feet. He felt strange. The bottom of his feet felt the cold of the floor, something they hadn't been accustomed to in a while.

'Looks like I've finally got you on your feet, but why stand when you can fly?' the voice cackled playfully.

'I'm not particularly fond of heights, and if you would have noticed, these pigeon appendages aren't really of great help.'

With his hands, or wings to be precise, Aryan strutted around the centre of his room in uneven circles, or at least what he considered was the centre of his room.

His attempts at making perfect circles, however, were a complete failure as he now seemed to be pacing about in a strange elliptical pattern, but to his credit, he wasn't really intending to pace his room in perfect circles.

'Why would I consciously try to pace the supposed centre of my room in circles? Is it not enough that I have to deal with problems like wings and voices and talking clocks?'

Even though he spoke of nuisances he had to deal with, there was a complete lack of any emotion in his voice.

'Now you have made me conscious of my pacing. How am I to think now with my mind and all the voices in it trying to compel me to create perfect circles?'

Aryan continued pacing—this time, however, with a lack of thought and a rather annoyed look on his face. He ensured he did not dwell into the darker crevices of his room. The thought of accidentally meandering into the empty black of the distant boundaries of his space, if it had any, scared him. He preferred leaving the far reaches undiscovered.

'What might give you the illusion that this room belongs to you?'

Aryan was a little surprised, but of late, he had begun to be able to manoeuvre his replies around these unnecessary and symbolically insignificant questions, unless of course the existentialism issues the universe faced had any relevance to his thoughts.

'Is there someone claiming ownership over this darkness?' replied Aryan, feeling rather smug. He placed his head in the cup of his two palms, making a sighing sound. The silence that ensued gave him the assurance that unfortunately no one was interested in being lord and master of his dingy room.

Aryan wasn't afraid of darkness as one would assume on first glance or, to be honest, upon any glance. On the contrary, he quite enjoyed darkness. It made him feel human.

Darkness deceived the impurities of his mind and body. It made him feel more complete than was ever true. The void of darkness was the envelope his shattered ego took refuge in. Darkness was strength, a place of solitude.

This strength was a tale true to days in the distant past, obscure like the dreamy paths of the universe.

'Darkness is not all solitude though. In the darkness lurk fear and other such monsters, few of which you have discovered. The monsters of the dark can be significant foes, especially to those with fickle minds and battered egos. In darkness there is refuge, and there is chaos. The darkness which was once illuminated by your ego, an ego you took pride in, now had dissipated into a vortex of indifference.'

As Aryan continued pacing the centre of his room, in time (as you would have guessed) in perfect circles, his thoughts had ceased, and his gaze dwelt into the darkness that surrounded him.

Around him was circle, the only illuminated portion of the room. He wondered if it would follow him wherever he went.

There was a whirring sound, like a very old motor coming to life after ages of abandonment.

From the darkness of the room a loud voice boomed, 'It's me, you foolish pigeon man. Me, Mikhail. Do us all a favour and stop with your curiosity. It's time to fly. I will not and shall not repeat—*it's time to fly.*'

Apart from a whirring sound which slowly ebbed away into the silence, all that gave Aryan company now was the sound of fluttering feathers, generated by a breeze coming from some undiscovered place.

'Coo . . .' said Aryan unappealingly.

'You can coo all you like, but now there is no way back. You have to leave me and move on into whatever rubbish awaits you.'

Aryan mustered up his courage. Why he was afraid of a clock, he couldn't tell.

'I want to leave you. This is not a matter of sorrow to me, and I am done with your pestering.'

The voice in his head spoke. It seemed dejected by the fact that Aryan had not acknowledged it.

'I too have a face, Aryan. You just never noticed. Goodbye, dear friend. We shall speak again.'

As the voice faded away into what seemed like a momentous silence, Aryan heaved a sigh of relief. He was finally alone; there was only darkness in his mind.

Aryan gathered up all his fallen feathers and arranged them in a neat pile in the centre of his room, probably his way of paying tribute to a room he never really enjoyed yet would hold in warm regard.

The clock yelped back to life. He sounded frustrated.

'You fool, you are going to return. They always do, there is no doubt of that. Now listen to me carefully. Comb your hair, mend your ways, for only the dwellers of the dark will be enveloped in the light. This is my last conversation with you, at least the last one till you return. Unfortunately for me, the mighty Mikhail, I also dislike your face and your mind.'

'I really don't like any of these people in my room. Why is everyone so vague?'

Aryan decided he could not handle the excitement of his departure any longer, especially the way he was getting battered psychologically and metaphorically.

He walked forward. His wings had vanished. This could only be good, but as he reached the limits of the light circling his being, he realized he knew not where the door was.

'I knew not where the door was, splendid sir. You have already begun talking like a dead man before taking to the light.'

'I thought you bid me farewell.'

'Bid you farewell? I bid no one farewell. Mikhail comes and goes at his own terms.'

'It does seem as though someone sent you here though.'

'Shut, shut, shh . . . I have a ticking temperament, tick-tock.'

'Since you are here already, may I ask where the door is?'

Lokhvitsky's voice broke in dramatically. Everyone in the room was certain he had no idea what was happening, apart from the fact that he wanted to impress Mikhail.

'Afraid of the dark, are we, *boy*? Close your eyes. You will know what needs knowing.'

As Aryan shut his eyes, in the midst of gleaming light, he saw what he was yearning for—the door, the door that would lead him to majestic dreams and realities beyond belief.

Slowly and cautiously he walked to the door, gazing at it with all his might. He felt no particular emotion, which again did not really amaze him because that would be feeling an emotion towards not having any emotions, quite a humorous irony.

'The dwelling of my soul, the residue of my ego, the universal diaphragm of thought, the sooty sinew in my veins, all concealed within this terminal door.'

'Yes, *yes*,' yelped the voice in his head. It was back, brooding complete.

'To open would be a great folly. Indeed it would!'

There was a quiet gasp, as though the voice in Aryan's head had found some reason for him not to abandon him.

'A contradiction to your philosophy, to resist would be to persist!'

Aryan was too lost in his battle to care for the voice. He did feel its desperation, and he quite enjoyed being in a dominating position for once.

'I am a mortal man with an immortal decision.'

'Ahh . . . finally, the pigeon man speaks like a true benefactor. I almost believed all this effort I had taken to convince you to walk through that door was in vain, and yet it still is.'

Mikhail seemed pleased with the development in Aryan's confidence.

'Do stop calling me pigeon man, Mr Mikhail. I think it is rather derogatory.'

'So it would seem, but in the progression of time, you will know what I mean.'

'I do not have a remotest doubt this is absolute chaos, but only time will tell.'

'Do not speak so idly of time, it is your only constant. I do not know if it is your past that will one day tell you of your dreams of the future, but one thing is for certain, your present is absent.'

'All this random talk, and now look, the door has disappeared. Maybe I should take a nap, and it will reappear.'

'Yes, yes, do take a nap. Hopefully that darned door has shown his face for the last time.'

The voice in his head sounded desperate now. It really didn't want to be left behind.

'I don't understand why you are so adamant I don't walk through that door. Mr Mikhail said himself that I would be back here!'

When Aryan awoke next, he sensed a lot of impatient bystanders—the clock, the chair, the radio, and a silent voice, which even without saying a word made its presence felt quite formidably.

'I was just going to awaken you with one of my more popular tunes.'

'Oh yes, please do, please do!'

'Quiet, Lokhvitsky, before I wipe that grin of your silly face.'

Aryan was laughing; their conversation was amusing him.

'He's inside a radio, which would be quite an improbable task!'

'To you he is a voice in the radio, but to me, what he is and what he isn't you will never know.'

'That was beautiful, Mr Mikhail, so deep and enduring, like time itself.'

Followed by this statement by P. A. Lokhvitsky was the resounding sound of what seemed like an extremely hard slap.

'Ouch!'

'You realize now the difference between our dimensions, my dear friend. For me, Mikhail, nothing is impossible. That slap was on its way for some time now.'

Aryan arose and, with a determined face, walked towards the door, which now seemed to make no effort to conceal itself. It was quite a disappointment as a whole and held no grandeur. It was white and had on it bronze hinges, which were definitely rusted. The door could have been much taller than seven feet.

The door which was a giant rectangle was subdivided into two smaller rectangles. The rectangles were rounded with what seemed to be barely any craftsmanship.

It was covered with a cheap hazel-coloured oil paint, or so it would have appeared to an ordinary (or in Aryan's case, slightly unordinary) bystander.

The subtlety of this door gave Aryan great delight, and what truly graced his conscience was that it did not speak back to him.

It was just a simple door, chipped and cheaply painted.

'This door is a perspective of the fear in your being, Aryan, since you possess no soul, and personally, I do believe this entire soul business is all hogwash.'

For once, Aryan agreed with the clock. Maybe he was brainwashed. As expected this statement went completely unanswered and ignored. Aryan turned towards the talking clock; on his face was a smug smile. Mikhail knew immediately this did not bode well for him. Throughout history he had been battered and bruised by men who had given him this very same smug grin.

'Don't even think about it. You are bound to me by destiny. I am your creator, I am your time. Look here, Aryan, look at me. Might you get the urge to discard me, you will be lost forever . . . Forever you will be the—'

There was a loud smashing sound, followed by the reverberations of a spring being detached and bouncing away into some dark corner of the universe.

'Oh, timeless man . . .' There was silence.

'Bravo, Aryan, bravo. Mikhail was the ideal benefactor of that fate. Now there is a message for you, my friend, and I think this one you will like.'

'Only if Mikhail could have heard you, Lokhvitsky, only if.'

There was silence, a brief unnerving one, followed by the much-awaited white noise, which broke into a voice. The sound of her voice created a deep reverberation within Aryan; for once, the echoes of his conscience went silent.

A silvery yet orotund voice cut through the diamond of silence that had penetrated Aryan's plagued mind.

It felt like water flowing through the sands of a timeless desert. Aryan absorbed it all, yet he knew within a moment it would not exist.

'In the silence of your conscience,
Dwells restraint,
In the chorus of your chaos,
Dwells my being,

Come remain my vision,
Into the light,
For into darkness we fade.
I swear in the clouds I see a beginning,
I promise in the sun I see a dream.'
'Don't go . . .'

Aryan's inner voice showed angst he had managed to envelop within his being very preciously up until this moment.

'You have found something you lost and yet your grip is too tight. Remember, water and air will wander, so will your dreams. You cannot trap that which is not yours. Calm now, soon we will go search . . .' Her voice tried to revive a memory in his mind. He did not question it. He could hear her, yet time stood still.

When Aryan's gained consciousness again, he was seated on his chair. He could hear the broken dial of a clock whirring away rather painfully in some distant corner of his discovered room.

As he felt the warmth of his own being, he realized he was completely naked.

Upon first gaze, it would seem that he was of ordinary build, but upon looking closely, one could realize how emaciated he truly was. There was total lack of subcutaneous fat, and it almost seemed as though the fatigue was causing him to waste away. The veins beneath his sinewy skin were clearly visible, and the slight heaving of his skeletal chest gave him the appearance of a man diminished with fatigue.

His face, however, showed no signs of this emaciation; his eyes had a sparkle in them. The creases on his cheeks gave him the impression of a man who once was generous with his smile. The paradox of face and body showed his dwelling conscience and its struggle to grasp the concepts of universal illusion and reality.

It wasn't a special face. It was a face one would forget but not the story it spoke of. It felt to Aryan as though he had been dormant for an unfathomable measure of time. He had lost grip of what was illusion and reality. The voices around him had gone silent, and his mind had no opinion.

'I have gone nowhere, my dear friend. I was simply dwelling in the echoes of your agony. Have you not forgotten that I am you and you are me? I will forever haunt you, in your happiness and sorrow.'

There was a sense of relief in Aryan's conscience and physical being as the voice in his head emanated through the void.

'I'm glad you are happy, but why are you not dressed? Rather inappropriate, don't you think?'

'What time is it?' Aryan barked rather rudely.

'Oh, so your inner voice is only for the one you lost, isn't it? With me it's all command and demand! It has been but a fraction of a moment since your encounter. However, that is in relevance to the universal measure of time. I would have told you, had you not very conveniently smashed Mikhail.'

Aryan was glad the voice was back, but he really wasn't ready to reply to its banter. He was still pondering over how her voice had silenced all around him. She had caused his void to truly be what it was meant to be in its unadulterated and pure form. The chaos in the abyss had been silenced by the pathos in her voice.

To dwell with such rigid intensity upon another's conscience frightened Aryan. He had grown to avoid and abandon all reason and sound. Her voice changed all this; it was as if her words had modified the very dimensions of his conscience, moulding him into a being he had not witnessed since he first truly dreamt.

Who she was and what she meant did not matter. Aryan was scared yet wanted more.

'Fear, my dreamy friend, is constant. It is a divine universal motive to keep us from dwelling to deep within our ego. Fear is our friend, keep him close.'

'Why are you always a part of every thought I have?' barked Aryan, miffed yet amused at how no thoughts could pass within his void without a comment of some sort.

Aryan sat up from his chair. Moonlight trickled through some crevice in the far extremities of his room, illuminating his chest. He could see grains of dust dancing in the moonlight around him. The trembling light made him shiver with cold.

Ironic, he thought, how what is meant to create warmth was now causing him to tremble like a leaf in an autumn breeze.

'The light gives you the impression of a man who was once whole. This would make a great photograph. You look like a poor plagued man with no dreams.'

'Is this meant to make me feel better?'

'It's meant to make you feel cold, my friend.'

'The moonlight is freezing my soul.'

'We have no soul. We are the hollow man, the timeless man, the soulless man.'

Aryan knew he possessed no soul, yet as he lay upon the chair, gazing at the moonlight freeze his being, he felt there was something warm within, slowly dying.

Was he truly so diminished that he could feel the passing of his infinite? Aryan felt cornered. The concept of absence was too strong for him.

'To escape this cold gaze is near impossible, fool. Why do you fear what is inevitable? There is no place to go. We must dance. We must sing and accept the darkness of light.'

The voice in his head had returned to its usual demeaning self, threatening and demanding.

'You have become rather negative, though you still do not have that haunting presence that would truly intimidate me. Your voice is quite drab, I must say.'

As Aryan turned his focus away from the incoherent babble, a chill ran down his spine. It was as though his physical being had been asleep and now had awoken to the discomfort of the cold moonlight and had decided to rather unpleasantly send electric signals along the wavelength of his spine to make him remember its presence.

Aryan, accepting his body's turmoil, sat up straight. The light had very conveniently moved away from his cold gasping chest and settled itself upon his side table. The white gleamed in the moonlight basking in her cold darkness.

Upon the side table lay a parchment, the green ink on it illuminated with fiery intensity. His arm quivered, for Aryan knew for certain that these were a fragment of his thoughts. What they were doing on top of the side table he could not understand.

He had put them away. They were lost forever, for his dreams to resurface with such prompt and unscrupulous behaviour did not amuse him.

He was not ready. The parchment lay there, never once taking their steely gaze off the trembling Aryan. It seemed to him as if the parchment was pining for his attention and, at the same time, making sure his fear for it was not diminished for the minutest passage of time.

The parchment was piercing his mind; it was interested in his dreams.

The voice appeared interested. It could feel Aryan's anxiety upon seeing the paper.

'We are never ready, are we? Come, let us read a few meandering thoughts you have experienced: "I am not what you perceive me to be. What I am to become is not who I am while I write this. Even as I scribble these words, I can feel the change. The dimensions of my mind are being stretched and crushed at the very same moment. I cannot describe what it is that I am experiencing, for my mind forbids me to do so. I am a prisoner. I will perish. You must find a solution."'

'Quick, go to the end.'

Obeying Aryan's voice, there was quick ruffling sound of pages being turned. 'I am happy. This is what I wanted. There is no solution. The chaos of the universe has been muted.'

Aryan opened his eyes with a jolt. His body was drenched in sweat. There was something amiss here. There was a sound of loud swirling in his head, all thought passed. His eyes went cold like glass, and all expression was lost from his face.

'*Coffee*, please.'

All it seemed was forgotten. He knew what he had just endured yet chose not to think of it. There was a refrain in his mind he had not felt before.

'Coo . . . It's time to clean up, I suppose.'

He was surrounded by shed feathers, a rather annoying afterthought of constantly transforming into a bird and back into whatever he could be described as now.

'It is I, the mighty Mikhail. You may break me and ravage me like a thousand before you, but I will only return stronger.'

Nothing of what had occurred surprised Aryan; it was as though his mind had been tuned to anticipate the arrival of the talking clock.

The fact that he had shattered it previously seemed a distant and rapidly fading memory, something that had occurred in a universe he had travelled in once, well versed and yet abandoned.

'*Pigeon*, insignificant insect, your feathers are shed. The door awaits your demise, but remember, you shall not pass into the dreaded oblivion which you crave for with so much angst. I will make you suffer, *boy*.'

Aryan's glassy gaze did not falter. He heard distinctly. He obeyed. Aryan's hollow eyes drifted into the dark distance.

'Demise, such a beautiful thought,' Aryan muttered, his voice almost completely muted.

'Wake up, my friend. Do not be a slave. We are not servants to anyone.'

The voice in his head was fearful. He didn't want Aryan to be overpowered, for then he too would be lost.

'You dare disobey me.'

The booming voice of Mikhail resonated through Aryan's mind like a knife tearing through flesh. He was on his knees, and tears escaped his empty eyes, moistening his dry cheeks.

'You are weak, but now I am here for you.'

Mikhail softened his voice. 'This is like a game of chess. I do this only for your benefit. I would never harm you intentionally.'

The sudden change in Mikhail's voice brought comfort to Aryan. He felt warm.

'Don't you see what he is doing?'

There was another much stronger jolt of pain, and now Aryan was writhing on the floor in agony.

'Quiet, I do not need you. Mikhail is right, leave me.'

The pain dried up instantly, like the thirsty sands of a desert absorbing water.

'Rise now, timeless man. It is time to leave.'

Aryan's attention was dwindling. His focus had abandoned him. His eyes were sleepless, and mind aged. Nothing seemed clear. Voices were morphed and slow. All thoughts had abandoned him, just white noise and constant antagonizing pain.

He knew he must head towards the door. It had been in his presence for a countless measure of time, but he was yet not certain the time was right, even after the forced coaxing of the mighty Mikhail.

'This is my only way out,' gasped Aryan.

His chest was heaving now; he could feel his body slowly fade into nothingness of the void.

Aryan sipped on a smouldering cup of coffee, which he had craved for subconsciously, he supposed.

Most of his cravings within his subconscious were satisfied by an invisible energy, but all his universal paradigms and their complications towards him remained unanswered.

Spppfff! Aryan spat out the coffee. It was horrible.

A voice echoed through the white noise. It was probably Mikhail or the radio—he really couldn't tell. 'It is I, Lokhvitsky. Why prolong? The time is now still. Only your departure will restart her constant.'

Aryan sat in his chair, observing these commands. Every time a voice penetrated words into his echo, there would be clarity in the white noise.

However, this also depended on whose voice it was. Ever since the grand Mr Mikhail had made his presence felt in the room via the clock, all other voices had lost domination, especially post the period when Aryan had smashed the clock against the floor, shattering it into pieces.

All other voices now had gone silent, only pain accompanied Mr Mikhail's voice, no taunts or jabs from Lokhvitsky or the voice in his head.

'This, boy, is respect. The silence displays respect.'

'Feels more like fear to me.'

'Fear cannot be felt, it is imbibed. You will know the meaning of fear soon enough. He is one who loves to befriend.'

Aryan was in no mood to be stabbed with pain again, and he kept silent. He could feel every breath the fabric took under him. The hair on his arms rested on the smoothly polished surface of his chair. He could feel its heartbeat. His feet, resting on the cold dark surface below, felt warm. Everything seemed to be a contradiction in itself.

He knew for certain it was time to leave, for everything around him seemed to be dissipating, and he intended not to dissolve into nothing less.

Aryan rose and walked out of the door in the centre of the room.

6

Sparrows and Kings

It was bright outside; the sun was gleaming as brightly as it possibly could. In the sky above, there wasn't a single cloud, nor was there the faintest murmur of a breeze. All around lay dry leaves, yellow with thirst and crisp with warmth.

Aryan stood upon a cobbled pathway, meandering away into the distance. On both sides were tall trees which didn't cast a shadow. They seemed green and did not suggest for a moment that the dry yellow leaves scattered across the cobbled pathway belonged to them. The colours seemed much defined, giving the assumption that one was standing inside a canvas. The cobbled path had a strange violet colour, and between the crevices of the brick path was an intense growth of moss, a path that had not been treaded upon for a multitude of time.

In the distance, a small passerine bird chirped incessantly, very likely an old-world sparrow. It came from a height, and his call for female attention resonated around Aryan. His sound never for a moment left Aryan's presence, and the complete absence of a breeze left the initially melodic sound to stagnate around him, annoying him profusely.

Looking ahead into the distance, the path seemed to continue infinitely and, to Aryan, looked rather wet—a mirage or not, he couldn't tell.

As the chirrups grew louder, a thought that had often caressed his mind came back to hover over his confused mind.

'What is the need for the lonely bird to chirrup?'

There was silence for a moment as though the old-world sparrow was drawn towards this thought.

'Why this cry for attention? What need is there for this soulful yelp, a plea, a heart murmur maybe?'

He stood and then decided that maybe he himself should chirrup for a while.

He needed some attention too; maybe he, like the little lonely sparrow, would find himself a companion through the passing dunes of timeless chaos.

Aryan was not standing on the cobbled violet path any longer; the earth below him grew smaller and fainter. As his gaze turned to look ahead, he noticed how the path that had appeared to be curved was in fact not.

The turns were sharp and geometric, widest at the turns forming two dimensional cones.

It wasn't even close to being a predictable journey with a multitude of sharp bends and turns. The path vanished, and his vision was now replaced by the branches of a tree covered in pistachio-green leaves.

Aryan found it sublime how the path below depicted autumn yet here high above he seemed in the midst of spring.

The mix of yellow and blue, the warmth and the cool, came with the promise of a new beginning.

The lobed margins of the broadleaves were covered in drops of moisture which glistened like liquid gold as they absorbed and reflected the sunlight.

The dew perched at the edge of the obtuse leaf made it look like a goddess weeping tears of gold, trying to revive her dead companions who lay far below yellow and forever asleep.

As Aryan looked around, he saw perched on a crooked arm of the tree, the cause of the annoying chirrup.

It appeared to be a male Dead Sea sparrow. Although he had a grey crown, he bore it proudly like a prince. His neck was yellow on the sides.

It seemed as though he was wearing a reddish-brown overcoat and a grey vest within. All he lacked was pair of cufflinks.

Aryan flew through the thickets and sat next to the Dead Sea sparrow.

'Coo.'

This sound surprised Aryan. Being in such a bright setting, he expected himself to have transformed into a bird of slightly better manifestations than a dull grey city pigeon.

He despised being a pigeon, yet there he sat beak and feathers, cooing away in misery of his own degrading demeanour.

His greyish-white bill annoyed him further as it always seemed to be a part of his perspective which as a pigeon was quite forced.

'I wonder if all pigeons are upset about their appearance.'

He arched his neck, which was coruscating and had a reddish-purple iridescence along the length of it. The sparrow paid no attention to him. Aryan was not amused; he was no ordinary pigeon, and he was a rock dove and a domesticated one too.

He turned towards the Dead Sea sparrow, and standing on his reddish-pink feet, he gradually spread his wings out, trying to give an impression of grace and poise.

The black bars on his grey wings made him look rather ordinary though as he observed himself through his red beady eyes.

The sparrow turned towards him, looking a bit frustrated, and in a slow and rather muted tone, finally he spoke. 'Please stop.'

There was agony in his voice; it was a voice that could not be argued with.

'Apologies. What is your name?'

The sparrow gazed at Aryan. It was a piercing gaze. His red eyes seemed most and yet commanded respect.

'I am Urien . . .' Saying this, he turned his head away and continued gazing into the distance. His attention pointed towards something that was invisible to Aryan. Aryan simply stared at the regal Urien; he never imagined a sparrow to command a respect he was just bestowed with. For the moment, he decided to turn his attention away from Urien, who had now begun to chirrup again.

His feathers were rather itchy; another of those disgusting parasites had probably found its way into his grey insignificant body. The constant nagging feeling of being an insignificant pigeon had begun to bring him down, this time only metaphorically though. He could never convince his mind of the significance of his existence whether human or bird, and now

Urien just made it worse. As Aryan looked towards the mourning Urien, he knew he would not make an enemy of him.

Aryan, in his avatar as a rock dove, wasn't a very melodramatic person; he had actually grown to appreciate his transformative abilities. On this particular instance, however, Aryan was agitated. He flapped his wings and cooed irritably and, on a certain occasion, even managed to get a rather miffed and annoyed glance from his new companion, Urien.

He knew he had to be somewhere important, and he sitting perched high up on the branch of a tree wasn't helping this cause much.

His transformations had become rather reckless. It was as if the pigeon was gaining dominance on his human perspective, deviating and altering him. His feathers had begun to shed a lot too.

There was a movement next to Aryan. The regal sparrow seemed like he could not ignore Aryan's presence any more. He turned slowly and gracefully, poised all the time and looking regal as ever; his grey crown was shimmering in the sunlight that pierced through the green leaves surrounding them.

Urien looked upon the piteous pigeon which was Aryan and, in a slow yet dominating voice, spoke, 'Looks like pigeon has meandered into reckless waters and the timeless man grows faithless.'

If pigeons could show surprise, this particular pigeon would be the perfect example.

'Remember'—Urien smiled—'the river will flow.'

'You can hear my thoughts.'

'Your mind is noisy, but amidst the scatter, I heard your voice.'

Aryan was wondering why everyone could read his thoughts. It was quite a nuisance.

'Dreams come, dreams go, the mind remains. Minds come, minds go, dreams remain. Choose who you are.'

Aryan looked towards Urien, who had now turned his back to him and had continued gazing into the horizon. The silent skies got enveloped in a gentle breeze; Aryan could see the plumage on Urien stir in the summer breeze. His shedding feathers took flight around him.

'What is your story, Urien?'

'Every moment has a place in this blurry perspective we call life, for now, you must look, and I must lament.'

Aryan agreed that since he was already perched on a tree, for once not an inconvenient and unnecessarily precarious position which varied from the likes of electric wires and lamp posts, he might as well contemplate what lies beyond the horizon.

Urien's words had created a sense of satisfaction in his curiously hesitant mind. Aryan in this moment knew he was satisfied.

'I shall accept that in this moment I am a satisfied pigeon.'

Since he was satisfied, Aryan, the rock pigeon, decided it was time to move on to far more pressing matters. There lay a small obstacle though; he couldn't remember what these pressing issues were.

As Aryan pondered over his most recent future, he heard in the background the chirrup of Urien translate into a melodious and sorrowful echo of a voice.

'Deep in a darkened dream lived a prince. His eyes were made of gold, and his heart was diamond old. From within this darkness, there arose a lie. Forever his fate sealed grey and dry. One night, the dreary prince ate his frozen rice steaming like ice.

'There was a growl. "To whom might this cave belong? Is it just another forlorn tomb?" "It is mine," said the prince, standing proud not tall. The beast, with his gleaming eyes, trembled wild with delight. "Give me your soul so I may dine tonight." "I have no soul, just a heart gone gold." "I am a beast, and all men have souls." Even princes who are diamond old. The prince trembled . . . The prince believed . . . Then the beast's eyes gleamed once again; they were dark like coal. "Beast, so you do remember me. You once claimed what was mine." A tear glistened in the beast's eye. So it is true then. "Now I am man, and you are me . . .""

Aryan looked at Urien, who still had his back facing him, his head bent low.

'So you are a prince. You speak of tragic times.'

'All times are tragic, all moments hollow.' His voice was sullen like the summer breeze caressing a dry meadow.

For as long as time could hold her breath, there was silence. All they heard was each other's breath—no meandering thoughts, only silent chaos.

A golden light penetrated through the green ambush of Aryan's visions. The sun was moving. Time was truly passing in this moment. This was a moment that elated Aryan. He felt alive. He knew the meaning of the passing of life again. For as long as Aryan could remember, he had been betrayed by time, and now there she was, as beautiful as the golden light itself, natural and real. Aryan watched as Urien took flight and vanished into the horizon. It was a beautiful sight.

'It reminded him of her light-blue eyes he used to gaze into . . .

The feel of her dark tangled hair . . .

The whisper of her gentle laughter . . .

Her journey was now his.

He would walk to the inverted city of dream.'

Urien's voice resonated in Aryan's head and then went silent. Aryan gazed at the light in the distance, illuminating the light-blue sky above. He without knowing knew. There was a stirring in the path below. It seemed as though he had progressed a distance while being perched on a tree. The scenario far below had changed. The colour of the street was now of a deep-purple hue, somewhat resembling a purple coneflower. The dry yellow leaves had vanished, probably swept away by the breeze that had given him and Urien the grace of her much desired company.

What got Aryan's pigeon mind to truly take notice though was the slightly arched figure of a boy facing his back towards him and standing on the path far below. The figure just stood there under the tree where Aryan was perched. His gaze was directed to nowhere in particular. Aryan knew who he was, obviously; he could recognize his frail self anywhere. To look upon oneself from so high above gave one elevated perspective and quite literally too in this scenario.

Urien's voice echoed, 'The clarity of the universe can never be truly doubted, for it doesn't exist. The universe is a paradox. To dwell in the silent sorrow of a Dead Sea sparrow is reality. Chirrup till your throat aches. Without true desire, the void is bound to make an interpretation of your chaos and eventually give forth something beautiful. Thoughts like this only pollute the clarity of the non-existing constant. The dweller's paradigm, this is where we belong.'

Aryan looked upon himself far below, the strange haunting voice echoing all along in his mind. It was an eerie voice. It sounded hollow, yet there was more depth to it than any he had heard before. It was as if for once the very universe was trying to communicate to him directly, no mediums involved. He knew it was Urien yet wasn't.

'The universe does not complicate. No words are necessary for her to describe her emotions. The void does not speak. She only dreams and shows. It is us pitiable mortals who need words to dwell upon our stark and insignificant expressions.'

Aryan looked confused. He did not understand if he was being addressed or his hunched self far below standing alone while dry leaves floated in and out of his vision. The voice floated all around. He was quite certain this was Urien's doing.

'You think too much. We shall meet soon.'

Aryan looked towards his figure, now blurry; the intensity of the words and the varying emotions was getting to him.

'Listen to her words,
They dwell like hollow songs,
An echo in chaos, an onset of dawn,
Deep in a dream, he heard a voice
She spoke of light,
Yet in her eyes,
Lay only darkened dreams,
Two pearls in a milky sky,
Two gleaming drops in a misty sea.
When winter came, her light would shine,
The eagles soared, the magic died . . .'

The voice drifted away with the warm summer breeze, leaving Aryan with a tinge of anticipation and a growing sense of angst. Spending what seemed like eons in a room with a multitude of characters constantly bickering about unattainable egos, Aryan wasn't accustomed to the warmth of such comforting voices and visions.

'There lies within the labyrinth of these beautiful words a trap.'

Aryan was breathing heavily, almost gasping for breath; he did not expect his body to react this way. The outburst seemed to him rather unprovoked, yet he could not stop the anger from taking possession of his fragile rock dove body, and the words seemed as if they were almost forcing their way out of his beak.

'I am the timeless man,
No rising moon can deny me my ego,
I am not diminished by your words,
In every tree and every dying leaf,
Within every grain of sand and every breath of air,
In the darkness of the void,
To the sun and back,
My memory will haunt you forever,
The ticking of time,
The chaos of dawn,
None can deny me,
I am the timeless man,
Dreamer of the universe,
Master of none,
Yet within one,
Within all.'

The sweat on Aryan's brow seemed uncannily cold. His breath was almost absent. On, being looked upon by an onlooker, he would have given the appearance of a rather emaciated and surprised rock pigeon. He could not gain leverage on how those words escaped his mouth. There was still a loud buzzing in his mind, causing all thoughts of his own to seize. He knew that, even though the very words uttered poured out from within the narrow confines of his beak, it was not him speaking. It could not be, for if it were, he would have known why there belonged in his voice such disdain and towards which unfortunate sentinel of the universe it was directed at.

Aryan heard a sound, a leaf twitching, a branch bending—it was graceful. The breeze had passed; the air was still like a wild cat perched on her limbs, waiting for her prey. Aryan tried turning his gleaming blue neck in the direction of the sound, but he seemed to be paralysed. He was certain it was Urien but he needed to be sure.

'You humans and your necessity to always know, it amuses me.'

'How do you know I'm human when I'm perched here next to you with feathers and all?'

'Have you ever seen a rock dove sweat? Also, I can see into your mind. It is like gazing into a pond on a stifling summer morning.'

Aryan looked straight at his diminutive figure standing far below. He had given up trying to move his body, and it seemed like his human form below was quite satisfied not moving either. He did not know what the words uttered by the supposed Urien meant, but he wasn't amused. To Aryan, being a pigeon wasn't a pleasing thought. What annoyed him further was that when he had finally managed to escape the confines of a room, his being had yet again managed to surprise him, and not in a good way, by transforming into a rock dove, and what truly bothered him was the fact that he had no control of his motor functions any more.

Why could he not transform into a graceful Dead Sea sparrow like Urien?

'What makes you think that, unlike your unappealing alter ego standing far below, I too am not you?'

There was a pause. The thought that he really was Urien elated Aryan.

'Before you respond, let me tell you, because you aren't. You will always be a rock dove, and one day you will know why.'

Aryan frowned. Urien was mocking him.

'Someday,

Someday we will all pass into the void that you are so afraid of,

One day you will welcome it with open arms,

You will know what it means to be free,

There ends your captivity,

Aryan, if you want the sun, you must die in the rain.'

Aryan had ignored most of Urien's words even though they had caused the shades of the dying leaves to change colour. He was quite upset he couldn't be Urien.

'Your words are of no value to me. You are like all the rest, invisible to me.'

'My words are just a dream for the dying . . . Forever will I be a fading memory.'

A pause haunted his eerie voice.

'Now tell me, why, sitting next to me, do you brood over ego and death when gazing into the dreamy skies you see her eyes? Embrace the chaos.'

This last statement Urien said in a rather chirpy voice. It seemed almost as if all his past brooding had been replaced by a new-found desire to confuse the rock dove seated beside him.

'All I want to do is go for this event. This event where I am assuming all my realities will come alive, but clearly, it would seem like my ego would rather have me sit here for all eternity, listening to the non-specific ramblings of a schizophrenic Dead Sea sparrow who does not know if he is brooding or happy.'

As Aryan continued with his outburst, his feathers slowly and not very steadily started dissipating from his body.

'Look, Urien, you've got me all upset now, and my feathers are shedding. How do you expect me to get down now?'

'Aryan I am one with the universe. My desires do not stagnate with the isolation of my thoughts. They flow like a river.'

'I cannot do this. I do not know whom you speak of. I will not entertain you. This must end . . .'

'It shall . . .'

7

The Perspective

Followed by what seemed to be an infinitely long blink, Aryan's eyes opened. Cobwebs drifted aimlessly in and out of his perspective as his retinas tried frantically to adjust to the rather exaggerated quantity of light passing through them.

A fascinated Aryan tried to focus on these floaters, but they never seemed to stop drifting. As he followed their movement, his eyes fell upon his feet, and to his surprise, they weren't bird appendages. He now stood on the street below the tall tree he had looked upon for so long.

His perspective had changed; he was back to being a human. Aryan felt relieved. He could feel the heavy thud of his heart as it pumped blood to and fro in his body and with what seemed to be quite an effort.

He felt the ache in his arched neck, not having been moved for an immeasurable amount of time. He could feel his trembling knees exhausted from holding his body in an upright position, barely supported by his hunched shoulders. Yet the featherless Aryan was satisfied. He knew now that his journey would continue. As he turned around and gazed up into the tall tree behind him, he saw there a rock dove and a Dead Sea sparrow gazing back at him.

'There is no bending of time, the lonely universal constant.'

The thought generated immense sorrow within his being. A sense of agonizing melancholy welled up within the hollow, gaping void that was his body. It seemed as if sorrow was flooding his thoughts and engulfing his dreams. Was it the varying words of Urien, or was it more? Only time would tell.

There was a sudden rush of wind. It wasn't the kind of breeze that one would enjoy while walking down a sunny path on a timeless evening. The air was studded with shrapnel, hurting and stinging. The skies above were darkening. Night was approaching and rather rapidly too. Aryan had forgotten the pendulum of time. Even in perspective, it existed, and now it was swinging towards him faster than ever. His conscience understood that.

He could not return to where he started. Haste was of utmost importance. Everything seemed to be happening rather rapidly. His pounding heart grew louder, and his breathless heaving grew hoarser. Aryan was spinning in circles, yet he saw clearer than ever. There was something pulling at his legs and arms, yet he could not see who, which to him was not surprising. His visions were shooting visions of blinding white light, causing him further angst and pain. Then there was loud screeching sound accompanied by a stabbing jolt of pain he had never experienced before. As the shrapnel in the air grew sharper and the wind louder, the seeping pain engulfed Aryan completely. His feeble feet gave way.

Aryan lay gasping on the floor alongside a pile of decaying autumn leaves. He heard them crumble and dissipate under his almost lifeless body. A voice howled through the misty haze of dawn that had replaced the bright day. It caused him to tremble with fear.

'This is no ordinary pain,
Your soul is dying,
Our soul is dying,
She is taking her last breath,
I can see visions, visions of a departing soul,
Yet all is not lost,
There is still time . . .'

Aryan knew this was the voice he had been waiting all along. Beyond the agonizing pain, he knew it was finally happening. The voice vanished, the trees dissipated into nothingness, and his pain seized. Aryan was always breathless, but this was different. It truly felt as though something had died within but not completely. He believed the voice, yet he could not accept that it was his soul, for he had none. There seemed something vaguely familiar with what was occurring to him. Aryan sensed familiarity, yet he couldn't have been further away from discovering why.

'Life is like a fleeting dream,

There are smiles and tears,

You will have regrets,

Only memories add unfulfilled desires . . .

No dream fades into life . . .

It ends . . .

As you see your dream tread into darkness,

So will life.

This is all.'

The pace at which everything was occurring frightened Aryan. He had no memory of such emotion; it almost made him feel human.

As he blinked and tried to get of the dark pavement, his eyes stung from the onslaught of the intense shrapnel-laden air that has reduced him to a trembling mass on the purple path below his currently trembling feet.

'I never want this pain to stop. This is utopia.'

As the pain began to fade, getting suppressed at the back of his mind somewhere, Aryan knew for certain this was how it was going to be from this point on. All that endured from a ceaseless pain was a gentle throb in his hollow midriff region. His soul seemed to be dissipating, squirming in anguish, as it slowly died.

'This is no ordinary end, my friend,

Your soul is dying with you,

There shall be no essence when you fade into darkness,

There will be no shadow beyond your dreams,

Only darkness.

Your soul is an abyss.

Void invisible.

Your energy is not dissipating; it is disintegrating.

This, dear friend, is the death of you.'

Aryan trembled as the voice echoed in his mind. It was a clear voice. A voice he loved and despised.

'You will follow my voice into the void, from darkness to light and back.'

'You are a real pessimist, aren't you? You only talk about my death and other such negativity, yet for some reason, you assume my essence is enriched by your presence.'

'I am a part of your essence, only you do not recognize me, but soon you will know who I am.'

There was a glassy silence, a kind of silence that would endure in the void.

'You shall cease to exist,

Not even your energy will survive,

Falter through the night,

For your energy diminishes through the brightness of reality,

This, my dear, is your fate.'

'I do not believe in the concept of a soul. It makes no sense to me. However, my energy ceasing to exist completely does frighten me. Is it necessary for you and everyone to be so sceptical about my existence?'

There was no reply, so Aryan continued, 'Suppose I did possess a soul. Why must it perish with my body? What happens then to my dreams and illusions? Why must I not have the fortitude to suffer the fate of every other individual around me? Why am I destined this fate?'

Aryan was the benefactor of a rather straight face as he spoke these emotion-filled words, for he really didn't know who he was speaking to. He also knew Urien sat above, gazing at him occasionally. He did like Urien a lot even though he had had some differences with him before he had returned to his human form. Aryan did not want Urien to notice him talking into the cool breeze floating around him and judge him, yet he spoke to Urien.

'Do you see a lot of individuals around you?'

'It was a rhetoric question. You really didn't need to answer it. Also, yes, that was my next question. Why am I always in isolation? Why am I not graced with the company of other humans?'

'Do sentinel beings not suffice? Do you consider yourself superior?'

Aryan was losing function of his facial movement. It seemed as though the energies around or within him did not approve of his incessant questioning. Through the rock dove's perspective, Aryan still stood motionless, gazing into the dark pavement, yet through his own gaze, he danced with emotion, his rapidly numbing mind dancing with emotion, warped with smouldering sorrow. His eyes were almost completely shut now, and as his mind went completely silent, he heard the voice one last time.

'I am not negativity. You have questioned the working of the universe, and this is your punishment. I am Urien. I am your master. The inverted city lies ahead—your dream, your destiny.'

8

Pigeons and Paradigms

As on every occasion, when Aryan questioned the voices in and around him, he had drifted into a limbo and was now awaking from it. He was just recollecting what had caused him to drift into this agonizing darkness, but his mind was still numb, and all he could extract from the slightly conscious mind was his doubt of the pigeons. He really was very suspicious of them. The solitary gaze of the rock dove above him increased it further. Something seemed amiss. As he had turned to look for the gazing pigeon, he had noticed it was bright again, and no trees, leaves, or sentinel beings now gave him company.

He stood on a pavement which was now orange for some reason, and all around was a uniform grey. He dared not look into the sky, in which sparkled a sun surrounded by darkness, for if it did not exist, he was afraid it might alter his reality and take him back to the room. If this was a dream, Aryan did not want it to end. He decided that there was only one way to end this paranoia and distress his partially numb mind was applying upon his conscience, and that was by walking down the bright-orange pavement into the horizon ahead.

Even as Aryan walked along the orange pavement which had nothing but a haunting hew all around, he had a nagging feeling he was being watched. He knew some sentinel being was observing his movement and waiting in gloating silence to end his progress. Ahead of him, just covering the entirety of the pavement, was a transparent barrier.

It was rippling; it seemed as though a pebble had been thrown into it, creating beautiful reverberations on its surface.

Aryan knew he must walk through it, for his thoughts were already losing boundary, and even a momentary lapse in time might become an abrupt ending to his journey.

'Do you believe you will find the pebble on the other side?'

Aryan inhaled deeply, ignoring the voice. He stepped through the shimmering barrier. It was ice-cold. Aryan felt like his being had been frozen. The cold did not end as he stepped across either, and as he crossed the transparent barrier, everything on the other end was rippling—the pavement, his feet, and even the sparkling sun far ahead in the dark sky.

He saw no pebble. Aryan felt as though he was standing under water. His brain felt the same way. Thoughts were flowing slowly, and as Aryan had anticipated before, he crossed this unexpected yet rather beautiful barrier, there was a voice. It was his own.

'I am certain I am being watched by pigeons. It seems to me like they are beings of a much larger psychic dwelling peering through a universal wormhole and judging and enticing the doom of mankind. Their lazy demeanour is only a facade by which they pretend to go unnoticed. Within every man, there is a pigeon waiting and watching.'

A voice echoed through the silence. He had forgotten how she sounded.

'You can never go home again,

Angels have left you behind,

Never will you see them again,

You are mine, and yet I will never be yours . . .'

Tears welled up inside Aryan's eyes, yet he did not stop. He ignored her voice. He couldn't think of her. He turned his attention back to the pigeons as though she had never spoken.

'They have outwitted most dwellers, but I am smarter than they believe. I am smarter than all of you sentinel beings, and I care not for your eulogies on universal paradigms.'

He had to ignore her voice, yet it kept reverberating in his mind, comforting him, dragging him to some beautiful reality. Aryan did not remember whose voice it was. All he knew as he dragged his body through the rippling universe was that he must forget. He closed his eyes tight.

'I know you better than you can imagine, pigeons. Remember, I was one of you just recently as I sat perched high above rather uselessly.'

Her voice disappeared; the ripples vanished. All was still again. He could breathe. The path had straightened out, and the trees had reappeared. They, however, all looked identical, repeating into the distance. Every leaf that lay below every tree was identical, yet there was only one sun sparkling in the grey sky. Aryan wondered if the creator of this parallel lacked imagination, but he doubted it.

'Is this infinity?'

'Infinity is not easy to obtain, yet you are close.'

It was Urien's voice, and it was echoing. It seemed as though a multitude of Urien's were chirping at Aryan at the same time.

'Urien! You followed me through the shimmering barrier! I am almost glad to hear your voice.'

'It was a gateway, not a barrier. I never left you. Look carefully.'

As Aryan stared up at the branches of the identical trees, he saw on the same branch of every tree a Dead Sea sparrow and a rock dove gazing into the glassy distance.

'Tangled in a web of glassy dreams,
Under a blossom tree,
Hand in hand,
Someday we will find each other,
Memories and sorrow,
Dreams and destiny.'

Aryan stood, not knowing how to respond.

'Her voice will haunt you into darkness, Aryan.'

Aryan was grateful of some company, and even though Urien's physical being was repeated into infinite, he trusted his mellow yet commanding voice. As Urien's voice diminished into silence, Aryan noticed that the almost infinite perspective had now changed further. The trees and the orange path below his feet, along with all other elements, had been mirrored above, casting the sky out of his perspective and replacing it with an inverted image of what he saw ahead of him.

The sun, however, lay exactly where it was before, not being doubled. Aryan was afraid to look above him and see if his eyes would converge with his mirror image. It frightened him to think how, if their visions collided, his with himself, he might dissipate into some other parallel, losing track of his journey.

Everything was changing drastically. His parallel was losing stability. Aryan could sense impatience; maybe it was due to his own sense of anticipation.

'Do not give such unneeded credit to yourself, my friend. You are not even remotely capable of such intricate elegance. To fragment a universe like this is the task of a much greater sentinel.'

Aryan was a little taken aback by Urien's onslaught, but he believed him. Presently, all his mind could think about was the pigeon propaganda and avoiding his inverted vision directly above himself.

'Do you know what lies above you?
Only your shadow,
But do not look for even shadows belong,
Do not tempt the unknown.'

Urien's words were more than enough for Aryan not to look up, for he truly believed in the journey this parallel was offering to him. Also, he was afraid to return to the lonely room he had so long been an occupant of. As Aryan stared into the distance, he noticed at the convergence of the above and below a rectangular shape which looked a lot like a door. It was a shade of brown, and it seemed very enticing. Aryan figured that he must move towards this door before this already unstable parallel collapses completely.

'Walk now, for rather there is earth beneath your feet than endless voices upon your brow.'

'Well it's not like you're going to keep quiet if I began walking. If that was the case, I would have arrived at my destination far earlier.'

'My words are what guide you on. Whether you approve or not is only symbolic to me, for remember, I once told you, you are me and I am you.'

As Aryan began his walk towards the impression of a door, the intensity of the sun had multiplied, and it seemed to him as though it was attempting to char his already diminished essence. This he was certain was not a good occurrence, for it had already been made quite clear to him by Urien and whichever voice he was unceremoniously introduced to that his essence and he were to be completely erased from the dwellings of the universe, leaving no trace of his energy behind.

A charred essence would clearly not make a good impression on an already sceptical universe. Universal energies, as he knew, were very temperamental and quite biased.

'Everyone around,
Hear my plea.
All I want is the brown door,
All I want is a little touch.
My feathers have floated away,
My beak is in the way,
My eyes see only far.
Will I ever get near?
I was never promised much,
Yet here I am,
So why stop now?
Will I ever get near?'

'This is what we feared. The dimension you are in is too fickle. As you go deeper, your thoughts will grow weaker. There is no way out.'

There was warmth; it was one of those rare occasions where he could lament, speak, and not wake up in a different dimension, completely isolated from his previous thoughts. As the warmth spread, Aryan's vision meandered. He was within himself. Aryan gracefully drifted through his thoughts. It was beautiful to him. He was in his own mind, flowing through his visions. He was moving rapidly. He was up on the tree and then down below. He heard every conversation, he smelt every smell, and he felt every emotion.

Aryan was going rapidly through a waterfall of emotion. He was afraid to stop. There was anticipation; he was going to see what happened before the dark confines of his solitude.

He flew through the door of his room. He saw the talking clock and the radio. He saw his room in light and darkness, and then just as he was about to leave the confines of the room, he hit a wall, and there was darkness.

'This, dear one, is despair.'

Aryan truly felt despair, for he neither was he going back nor was he moving forward.

'Why do you desire to see what lies behind the darkness? How are you so certain it is better than this moment? The time is not yet upon us to dwell into your parallel reality that you so wish to unravel. Do you truly believe that behind the darkness there lies a universe you believe in? If such, is your belief then don't hesitate? For if you look carefully, you will see beyond.'

Urien seemed to know a lot about him. It gave him a sense of strength to know that there was a voice, even if it belonged to a sparrow, and that it was guiding him.

'Come, finish this journey. You must find her, the inverted city.'

'Why do you talk of inverted cities and me finding someone? It makes no sense to me.'

'You will know what I mean. Not so long ago, you desired a door, and now here you stand in front of another desire. This will never end, Aryan. This is only the beginning. This is the disparity of life, in one dimension or the next.'

Aryan opened his eyes, and there in front of him was the door, the door he so longed for. In front of him appeared a man. In his eyes, he saw patience. There was a tune in the air. It was her voice again.

'Sinister moons,
Dreamy eyes,
All my lies dwell within.
In strange tides,
Stranger lives.
There we were in the depths.
Beyond the trees,
Came shadows forth,
Yet all we did was stare,
All we did was wait.
Now time has passed,
All is dream,
Sinister moons,
Dreamy eyes.'

Her voice drifted through the palms of his hands. He could almost caress it, yet like a fleeting breeze, it disappeared.

There was a smile on the face of the man who stood between Aryan and the door. His eyes did not share this emotion. They were dark, like the ocean of the night.

'Who are you?'

The man spoke softly, a familiar voice indeed. 'Do you not recognize me, dear friend? It is I, Urien.'

Aryan believed him instantly, for there he stood as regal as ever. He had on his head a grey crown. The crown had on it three tines. The tine in the centre looked like a Scottish shield, bent like a bow, with a higher middle section. To this tine was attached a silver plate, and on either side of the plate belonged a crescent-shaped prong. At the periphery of these outer prongs were greyish-silver feathers, each feather twisted to look like a spiral.

The sun fell on them, making them glisten and gleam. No gold in the world could replace the sparkle they endured with. It was beautiful and subtle. The crown looked old. It looked like it had been the possession of many a king before it had found its way on to Urien's brow.

Like the Dead Sea sparrow Aryan had interacted with earlier, his human avatar in front of him had dawned upon himself a reddish-brown overcoat and a grey vest within. The only difference was the presence of cufflinks. Urien looked princely. His face was chiselled, and he possessed high cheekbones.

Of what was visible of his hair from under the crown, Aryan noticed dark tangled brown hair with a curled strand resting on his forehead. His skin was pale, and his brows strong and arched. His eyes were black as coal. His shoulders looked like they had at some time been the bearers of great burden. His face deceived time, yet his eyes spoke of older days. He possessed warmth yet looked as though he was the tormentor of souls.

'You are not the only one, my friend. I too sometimes have the unceremonious pleasure of fleeting passions.' Urien continued to smile. 'The crown belonged to the mighty halls of once-great kings. How it has found its way on to me is a story for another moment.'

Aryan was looking up and gazing into Urien's eyes now. He was listening to him like a child.

'So now this door that is behind me, do you believe it is in your destiny to walk through them?'

'I do not know if I believe in destiny.'

'Upon every brow rests a fate,

Within everyone lies a destiny,

Yet to embrace it, we must linger,

We must wait,

For destiny will find you,

Like it has in this moment.'

Urien looked down at Aryan, not expecting a reply, and he did not get one either.

His left hand was enveloped in a black glove, and in it, he held what appeared to be a sceptre, only it was wooden and looked rather ordinary. He looked at Urien one more time and tapped the wooden sceptre on the pavement below.

'There is a humming in the breeze. Can you feel it? Can you sense the clarity, Aryan? The paved road under you is at end. Change is upon us.'

Aryan was the timeless man. He had no perspective of time, yet he heard the ticking of destiny and felt the passing of spring.

'Let us go, my dear friend.'

Urien turned towards the door, pushed it open, and walked into the darkness. Aryan did not utter a single syllable. His mind had warped. He followed Urien into the black.

9

Dreams and Destiny

In the reminiscent starlight was a haze of reverberating life. She was swaying in the moonlight with a glow so eccentric; it was serene. A life of depth yet warm like a gentle summer breeze flowing within the boundlessness of a starlit night. Above her the constellations reverberated brilliantly, forever a guide to the lonely wanderer.

It seemed like the stars were glowing upon her, reminiscent of untold thoughts and unread desires. Was I just the calm of the night flowing through hazy thoughts and dwelling upon complexities of a realm undiscovered? I looked to the east; a wind carrying a gentle thought caressed my essence, casting within me shadowy glimpses of mystic realms beyond my reach. Living within a melancholy, the crescent moon cast a deep rein of sadness within all undiscovered.

Within me, a glimmer of sorrow dwelt in my almost unreal void. It seemed to me as if I had lived only to see my thoughts vanish into a mist of chaos yielded by fragrances of the unattainable. Was I to recreate what had passed as I watched my desires cast into nothingness and yet not void? Was I to smile as I saw, fragment by fragment, all my thoughts for her disappear?

A harmony melodious only to the restless grew within a heart craving to be noticed by the mind it serves. A strange wilderness had crept within my thoughts tarnished with unneeded weariness. Look closely, look deep, you are always what you can never be, a lost moment and an unkempt desire.

In the darkness, I was a night desperate to be heard, my thoughts echoing in the universe. See my eyes wander past her thoughts so easily understood, like a child of dreams uncertain. My eyes were pungent with the summer rain as they crept past your gaze. I never meant to wander into your thoughts up until now. I see it all; I understand it all, like a drop of water cast into holocaust. I saw her beautiful longing for thought.

Omnipresent, potent, and illuminated by a dawn for yearning, all I wished was to be one with her forever through the havens of shadowy realms. As she once gazed into the depths of my eyes, I realized her unturned desires. Her thoughts were calm; where was the chaos I once danced in, where was the ravaging of thoughts that are now replaced by darkness? Still numb and instilled in sorrow, the silence frightens my very essence. My eyes were numb with pain; were you truly there? For I could never seek you yet I felt you.

Uncertain desires, unattained dreams. You were the universe I was seeking to find, to lament to gain, yet you walked away into the still night, not turning back to let me see your gleaming eyes one last time. Steady now, a glance into the distant skies, a perspective to my realm, and you could have discovered me, brought my wandering soul peace. Now there is only void yet no solitude. The longing to discover and yearn returned, showing the illusions of a fickle life.

Look to the west; the mystic wanders, his knowledge in his feet, treading through darkness, illuminated by pulse unattained. My eyes wander into the dreamy west. Look deep into my gaze, for I see what you see, I dream what you dream, dreams of desire and longing cast by oblivion unattained. For longing shall pass and thoughts shall fade, but you will dwell within my thought, mystic wanderer from the west. I have dwelt in your dwelling. Never truly lost, only scattered into a multitude of thoughts, craving for shadowy glimpses of my past.

Unrelenting are my ideas, of magnitude so varied it defies my very identity, a thousand voices, a single soul. We are one yet within me such a multitude, every emotion reminiscent. I looked up, tracing the stars, searching, hoping to reignite my thoughts, so lost, so devoid; where wanders my craving, my lust for knowledge lost with you. Wandering through her essence, her thoughts were truly unobtainable. Tell me what you took from me, lost in an icy universe.

Am I to start again, like a child from a womb? Rising from the dead, what thoughts are these if lost so easily, wandering into hazy nights, throbbing with infinite dreams, gone? Seek my dreams, see them; I never thought to gaze into my mind like you did, clear yet hazy and ever present. Was I scattering unknown and devoid to retain what must be? Pragmatic thoughts replaced by a still magnitude, your reverberating calm. Now I am on my way, hair misty with soot, eyes numb with sorrow. Streets fly past, and the breeze is lost, emotions so deep lost forever.

My thoughts for you devoured in a flame, thoughts slowly getting charred by a dark fire burning away my desires, for I will never see you again, never feel you again. Our journey leads us in different directions; I stay still, and you move away. One day we shall meet again when we are one with the icy universe. Your breath, my only warmth, I feel it in my essence.

When do I stop? Where must I cease? I think of days spent with you in the Indian summer. My thoughts shall wander into yours as long as the sun casts a glow upon my gloomy brow. As you lay beside me under the starry skies, the moonlight illuminated your pale complexion, your silence merged my thoughts into a singular craving for you. The glowing crescent above stirred the hazy depths of my untamed soul. Like a blooming flower in a surreal spring, your presence cast me into an undiscovered blur of light and darkness. Look far into the distant skies as you lie beside me, for our thoughts are dispersing as one, divine interventions. Look up for one day we shall be gone; still our essence will dance infinite and sublime.

I was famished with hunger too true for my presence. Radiant, passing your warmth into my cold, within the icy depths of my singular thoughts, unfulfilled desires before and now a never-ending longing.

Only if time had stalled in the gentle breeze carrying the lost sorrows of the sea, flowing past your moistened lips as if to grasp your breath and caress your numb eyes one last time before wandering into distant lands laden with thoughts desiring you. Never was a word spoken, yet your laughter, soft and laden with life, told me everything yet I knew nothing, wandering alone in the mist now—strange, calm universe.

Will I ever see you again? For without your glow, I am lost in the unexplored darkness of mystic times, I am. No touch, incomplete liberation. Louder echoes, louder footsteps, searching for a friend, a follower in darker moments. It was cloudy; the moon covered in mist. The clouds cast a sorrowful glance into the night we will soon dwell in. The moon fades into the darkness. I know you will never feel the way I have felt for you, for I was just passing in your abode of dreams.

Goodbye, my friend, I hope the stars shine upon you on to the end of time, for they have abandoned me and my abode of dreams.

10

Puppets on a String

Grey skies above Aryan were crying now, yet a thin sheet of icy glass kept the drops of sorrow from being amidst his presence. The pitter-patter in the sky above conveyed their message.

The bright light dimmed, and all was visible once again to Aryan. He looked rather dejected for around him was nothing, just an empty room.

Nothing spectacular either, a grey floor, white walls, and a ceiling covered in drops of rain, gleaming like diamonds in the sky. Urien was observing his movements.

'If the light does not pass, all we will perceive will be clarity, making the purpose of life futile.'

Aryan heard his voice. He had forgotten about him; his dejection had distracted him. 'Life is futile, is it not?'

Urien turned towards Aryan and looked at him with a contemplative gaze. He noticed Aryan's dejection and waited for it to settle. On Urien's face was a vary smile. The slight crease on the edges of his lips gave away his age; the smile gave away his story.

'You shall see only what you perceive. Now close your eyes and open them again.'

Aryan obeyed, and when he opened his eyes, he saw in front of him what he had so deeply craved.

'Now you see, no journey is in vain, all absolutes alterable.'

Urien bowed down to Aryan, and as he arched his back up again, a shining golden sceptre appeared in his hand.

'Come, let us glide. Frivolous matters need our attention.'

All around Aryan was movement. Men and women all dressed in black robes and gowns glided around him, and on their faces were masks.

The floor was gleaming and cold like ice. The raindrops in the floating sky sparkled like tiny diamonds, and all around, the hall extended as if forever. No walls or doors, just infinity and mist.

It was a haunting vision, for no one looked him in the eye, yet he knew all felt his presence.

A jester ran amidst the bland black colour, dressed in bright orange. He wore a conical cap with three golden bells attached to the tip; they chimed, gracefully synchronized with his leaps and bounds.

All around, the figures floated, wobbling a bit yet not camouflaging any lack of grace.

'Here is the thing about gravity—she is quite an egoist. She is the mistress of our realm and beyond. She believes not in meaningless words and thirst quenching promises. Within us all lies her essence. None can escape, for we are illusions captive in the reality of gravity, bound both in dream and reality by her.'

Aryan looked towards Urien with a slight despondency, for the floating people had barely awakened his curiosity, yet Urien had already explained unnecessarily to Aryan about this gravity character and her unfriendly ways.

'Do not be upset about what is beyond your control. The entire concept of getting upset is quite upsetting and human for my liking.'

'You are human! You look human enough to me.'

'Of course I am human! It would be absurd to think otherwise.'

Urien followed this statement by a rather unceremonious cackle of laughter, perplexing Aryan.

'You see, Aryan, in this room, no thought truly belongs to you, and yet they all are yours. Your fate is sealed in a series of uncertain and yet very clearly defined series of events. It is very possible that you, like all of us here, are a puppet too, but only time will tell.'

At this moment, Aryan was quite bemused and really wished someone would appear and explain what all these really meant. As he desired, someone did appear, but he clearly wasn't who Aryan was anticipating.

It was the same jester who had run through the crowd, cackling, only this time he carried a flaming torch in his hand and seemed quite flamboyant about it too.

'It almost seems like an accident is due, doesn't it?'

As Urien completed his sentence, the jester hopped and flipped his agile body over towards Urien and very conveniently spat out a ball of fire which aptly went and settled on to Urien's grey crown and illuminated it in a blazing red ball of fire. Ignoring his burning crown, Urien turned with a very straight face and looked towards Aryan.

'Quite impatient, are we not?'

Aryan had a big smile on his face, for the sight of Urien's head on fire gave him no greater joy. He also enjoyed the fact that he was being held responsible for these rather hilarious turn of events. What Aryan did not understand was why the fire did not seem to spread. Urien seemed to carry the blazing ball of red fire quite fashionably as he strutted about almost as though nothing spectacularly hot was upon his head.

His words had annoyed him to a great extent, but this strut was an almost immeasurable quantum of his growing annoyance towards Urien.

Urien, with a casual swish of his sceptre, extinguished the fire that had illuminated his brow, leaving behind a lightly smoking yet perfectly intact crown.

As Aryan turned away from Urien, he noticed the jester had only just started with Urien, for now he was running through the graceful mass congregated in the grand hall, lighting various portions of their attire on fire.

None in the crowd seemed to mind, letting the fire rise and fall as it desired.

Some flames were red like the one that had recently inhabited Urien's crown, yet others were a multitude of colours, casting beautiful shadows into the otherwise bland hall.

The jester had now settled himself on a stool, setting various parts of his attire on various coloured fire with his illuminated staff.

His cackle, unlike the fire all around, had been doused, and now he seemed rather glum.

'Do you know why your mind is so silent and white, my dear friend? The flames have been motioned into a graceful path illuminating your footsteps. Some day, when you glance back at what has been, realities will parch your vision, and all you will see is a morbid world with neutered dreams.'

As Aryan tried to register what Urien had said, all went dark.

'It's almost as if no one here wants me to think.'

'Why does the darkness prevent you from thought?'

Urien's voice boomed through the mighty hall, echoing through the infinity.

As light reappeared and Aryan's vision settled, he saw the congregation facing their back to him. They all were suspended from strings, Aryan dared not look up, might he discover he was suspended on strings too. Their bodies seemed less human-like and almost two dimensional; all expressions, constant.

There was no breeze, but they swayed slightly, puppets on a string.

All colours had drained away; all fires, silenced. Only the distant jingling of the jester's conical cap echoed through the reverberating quiet of the hall.

'Look beyond the clouds. Therein lies your destiny. There it will end, and there it shall begin. Someday you will know of what I speak.'

Aryan looked straight ahead, and on a pedestal stood the grand Urien. He seemed to have grown larger in stature, and from his back sprouted out large sparrow wings.

Urien's gaze penetrated Aryan, and his smile calmed him.

'It's time for a story.'

11

Pigeons and Jesters

' The concept of a jester probably determined the very workings of our sporadic universe, and yet through time, they were ignored and mocked, a mere source of entertainment carrying no gravity of importance or significance. What we did not realize—and by *we* I mean *you*—was that this was all an act, a face the jesters put up to never be doubted of their true intentions. The jesters were the founders and guardians of the universe. Somewhere beyond our vision was a panel, a panel of founders deciding and juggling their way through the complexities of our universe. Every possibility, every illusion, every dream controlled by them, monitored by them, started and finished by them.'

As Aryan heard these words flowing out of Urien's mouth, he had visions of him as a young boy—long flowing hair swaying in the wind, his father tall and sturdy walking beside him.

There were shouts of joy and awe in the air as jesters did impossible acrobatics and juggled with flaming knives and bottles. There was awe and bewilderment in his eyes. He was completely captivated.

The vision of his father was only from shoulder below, so he could not recall if he had been as captivated, but he was certain of no other possibility. How a jester had so easily enchanted the souls of every being in his vicinity made Urien's story all the more true.

'It was easy. The simplicity of captivation by colour and trick was an already inbuilt characteristic of the human mind, almost like an entrapment.'

Aryan was spellbound.

'We were designed to be blind believers of the mad hatters. Now, as we all know, to every black there is a white, and eventually, even the power of the jesters would diminish with time, bringing forth other opportunist minds to snatch this power from their hands, for who controlled the universe controlled all.

'As expected, with the growing nature of the jester's thought, brewing in the murky darkness was anti-thought, for all must have balance. What the jesters in their power-hungry frenzy did not realize was that the more they created for themselves, the more negativity they brewed all around.

'To keep watch on man, the jesters created pigeons. All the pigeons did was dwell in the presence of man, serving no purpose and possessing no worth.

'It was foolproof, for man never understood their purpose and left them to themselves, and all the pigeons did was multiply and observe and keep watch. The pigeons were controlled by an alternate panel of cloaked jesters, the grey watch.

'Soon darkness spread within the cloaked immortals of the universe, and they segregated from the coloured, leaving them to fend for themselves.

'The only alternative left was for the coloured jesters to descend into our paradigm in physical form and ensure the cloaked immortals did not alter the power balance of the universe.

'Hence were born the entertainers, the omnipresent coloured men. They dwelt in the courts of grand kings and all men, powerful, entertaining, and always watching.

'This was the paradox to the existing. Hence existed two powers, the cloaked and the coloured guardians of the universe, overseers of our conscience, masters of karmic uncertainty, shadow warriors of time.

'However, as time passed and seasons turned, the universe developed her own conscience with the constant thought that passed through her. She developed a conscience that could perceive all others.

'Darkness crept over the universe, crippling the pigeons and jesters, forever making them prisoners of our realm. The time of the cloaked and coloured guardians was over. There was a time when all was not dark. The black vacuum of space was blue like the sea and green like the leaves of a tree in a spring morning. The universe had negated all, creating dimensions in infinity, all free and yet trapped.

'The human mind was meant to be the universe, but she perceived thought and morphed it, for all need power, all need strength. This was how all was created, and this was how all was meant to end.

'The universe was meant to be utopia, a paradox to some other murky parallel created by the jesters. No power and betrayal, just clarity and independent thought.

'However, with independent thought came independent opinion, thought that could question the universe itself. The jesters had not perceived this, the reason for independent thought being that the universe and her masters would not be pestered before every decision. For example, if you, Aryan, were sitting on a table with independent thought, you could decide what you wanted to eat for breakfast and not ask the energy around you.

'The cloaked guardians, however, were unhappy with this concept of individual thought, the reason being that they now had individual thought and could question the collective.

'The pigeons believed it was a folly to impart such great power upon a race of blind believers.

'The cloaked guardians believed that individual thought was what separated them from man, like master from sheep, and now one and all possessed this ability.

'Now the jesters couldn't really be blamed for this act, for individual thought was the reason for all that had happened, she being the true master.

'The moment individual thought had been created, she had plagued the minds of the mighty and transformed into the true master. This was a concept the very creators of the universe could not perceive.

'By making the jesters believe it was their own thought, she had managed to gain control of all mortal and immortal beings that plagued her universe.

'She was creating an army, the universe's first and last great war, for we are just a plague, forced inhabitants of stability. The very sky became a lie, and man created false gods, forgetting forever the story of the cloaked immortals, their true creators.

'What she did not realize was that soon man would grow so blind in the concept of a higher reality that he would forget the very concept of individual thought herself. Now we live in a universe governed by none. Imaginary power worshiped by all.'

Aryan was simply gazing at Urien, not knowing how to react. He really could not perceive the concept of pigeons being faithful guardians of the universe, especially since he occasionally transformed into one. Was he a cloaked guardian too?

'Within all our minds lie the pigeon and jester, waiting in darkness, waiting in light, one day hoping the universe will glow. Once again, dragons and mighty kings will captivate our dreams, for we are only sheep in a sea of thought. The universe is lost in a mist. There is no thought, only void.'

There was absolute silence as Aryan and all the floating audience around stared at Urien. It seemed for a moment as though none around had understood Urien's words. Then there was a tremendous outburst of clapping.

The audience wobbled mid-air, losing all grace and charm. Their hands were exactly where they were prior to the cheering, making Aryan curious as to where the clapping sound was coming from.

'Bravo.' Urien had quite conveniently appeared next to Aryan and seemed very pleased.

The jester was back. He jumped high into the air, did a few flips and bounds, and disappeared into the crowd quite literally.

After Urien's speech on the jesters and pigeons, he had gazed at the jumping jester with quite a sceptical gaze, probably the reason for him to disappear so hastily.

'What truly is gratifying is that once we are past certain illusions, the grandeur fades, and all appears grey, does it not?'

This was true; Aryan could not deny that, for even the jester had lost colour before he had vaporized into the crowd.

'The time is near for you to return, dear friend, for illusions appear beautiful for only so long before they pass into doubt and uncertainty.'

'Not there again, please. Not the room.'

'All is fading. Before you are lost, you must return. Much is yet left to talk about, much left to dream about.'

'Can we not speak here?'

'The jester must be forgotten. Let us not reignite a dead story. A dream can turn dark when folly caresses her path.'

'I like jesters.'

There was a loud cackle, and all went blank.

12

Mila

It was a beautiful morning.

A dew-laden breeze caressed the gulmohar trees, causing them to gently shed their fragrant yellow flowers. They almost seemed as though they were murmuring in approval.

As Aryan lay in bed, gazing out of his window, he couldn't imagine a more perfect day. A lone sparrow sat perched on the edge of his window, sill chirping her melody, carrying her beautiful song into the infinite universe.

It was going to be a great day. As Aryan got out of his bed and casually walked to his window, he saw her. Standing on his porch was a girl. She seemed lost.

She had an angular face, with a soft creamy complexion. The morning light caught in her dark tangled locks, giving them a lustrous glow. A single strand of hair fell across her pale electric-blue eyes. They gleamed like the sky in a dewdrop. Her long eyelashes arched slightly upwards, giving them a graceful catlike appearance. Her skin was pale like snow yet glowed; cheeks were flushed by the warmth around her.

She wore a spruce-blue sundress in railroad-striped voile. It was pleated at the waist with a wide neck and thin straps. It had a white lace lining at the bottom enhancing her bony knees.

Strapped to her back was a tan-brown backpack; her back was slightly arched.

Her feet were enveloped in cognac-brown round-toe Oxford shoes, which very elevated from the back by large stubby heels, making her appear taller than she actually was.

Even though she stood awkwardly with her toes pointed inwards and her arms dangling loosely, she seemed perfect; her clumsy appearance gave her grace like no poise could ever do.

Aryan noticed everything about her. His mind had drifted into silence, and all thoughts left his being. He could feel his heart race. He could not understand why, but he didn't try to control it.

'Hello. I found you.'

Aryan regained perspective to see her standing against his window, smiling at him.

Her soft white fingers rested on the dusty windowsill, which she didn't seem to mind. She was not nearly tall enough and was stretched out on her toes, almost peeping into the window.

'Hello.'

Aryan's face was flushed. He hoped she wouldn't notice. He wasn't accustomed to human contact, and she was the prettiest he had come across.

'How can I help you?'

She looked at Aryan, her head tilted slightly, and from under her palm, she removed a crumpled cut-out from a newspaper.

'Are you Aryan?'

Her voice was silvery and light. There was a slight hesitation in it.

'I'm here regarding your article in the paper.'

'Article . . .'

'Yes, article. You are Aryan, aren't you?'

'Yes, I am. The article?'

'I know it's a few months old, but I thought I should try anyway.'

'Your nails, they are turquoise blue.'

'Oh yes, I love the colour.'

She stared at her nails for a moment and then gave Aryan a gentle smile.

'Why don't you come around, and I'll open the door for you.'

She took her hands of Aryan's windowsill, leaving tiny fingerprints in the dust. Aryan heard the light tapping of her heels as she made her way around his porch towards the door. Aryan kept looking at her as she turned the corner. Like her fingers, her feet left a trail of footprints in the dust. He hadn't been out of his room in the longest time.

He was nervous; she generated a sense of anxiety in him that he hadn't ever experienced earlier. As he walked towards the door, Aryan looked at himself in the mirror. His hair was uncombed and shaggy; his eyes, sleepy. There was stubble on his face.

His white T-shirt looked like a rag, but this would have to do, for even while he was wondering what he could do to alter his appearance, she was already outside. He heard her tap the door lightly with her knuckles.

Aryan unlatched the door clumsily; he had almost forgotten how to.

Before the door was open completely, she had already stepped passed Aryan and turned to face him.

'Hello again, I'm Mila.'

'I'm Aryan.'

'I know. I read your article about you requiring a tenant. I really don't have any money to pay you, but I promise I'll stay only till you get a paying tenant.'

Aryan, for some reason, did not consider this request strange at all. His mind had already accepted her, and his face expressed this emotion.

'Yes, you can.'

Aryan knew she could sense his hesitation. It was almost as if she knew he wanted her to stay. His need for her was not derived; his voice made it clear.

'How wonderful.'

She stood on her toes. She was much shorter than him even with the chunky heels that supported her cognac-brown shoes and, holding on to his wrist with the palms of both her hands, gave him a quick peck on his cheek.

Aryan was flushed. Her lips were soft and warm; his heart pounded.

Before Aryan could reply, she had already made her way into the house and was peeping curiously into the two rooms which lay across from where they stood.

'I like your kitchen, and this room seems lovely.'

'That is my room, but you can have it I suppose.'

Aryan didn't care. He couldn't stop thinking about her. Her eyes, like the sky, had captivated his thoughts the moment he gazed into them. With a smile on her face and a dream in her eye, she turned and walked into her room.

The door shut behind her. He sat in his room, wondering when he would get to see her again. He heard her much later; night had fallen.

Aryan could hear her walking around the living room outside. She was trying to be quiet. The sun had set; the moon was casting her haunting gaze through windows.

He could hear her vain attempts in trying to be silent; he couldn't help but smile.

'To dwell upon thoughts was vain

Transgressing through the universe, there will always be echo,

Soon minds will merge, and then they too will dissipate,

Leaving nothing behind but lonely desires and empty tears.'

There was a knock on his door; he could feel her bony knuckles beat against it. His thought passed. He walked up and turned the doorknob.

She was looking at him with strange sincerity. They were the strongest expressions he had gazed into; it made him nervous.

'The moon is enticing me. Would you like to join me for a walk?'

'Yes.'

They stepped out of the room. The moon was nostalgic. It illuminated against her pale skin, and she was night, cold like the grey clouds above, silent like their trembling shadow in the silver night.

She could see him look at her, yet she looked straight ahead. There was a constant and gentle smile on her face, her red lips and flushed cheeks deceived the realities of night.

'Sometimes I feel like the night is so sincere and the moon nervous like me. I am always nervous, maybe that is why the moonlight trembles. She is like a mirror to me. She makes me tremble too in this restless night, like the leaves and the glassy water she shines upon.'

She looked up into the sky and laughed, her white teeth glowing. She was almost black and white, red lips.

It was a beautiful sound, silvery and clear, a companion of the night. When he looked at her as they walked, she looked straight ahead, still with her peculiar smile. He wasn't sure if he had imagined her. Were her words real?

'Why do you think the moon is a woman?'

'So you speak, because I am the moon.'

She was laughing again, this time delicately.

'What do you do?'

'That is a very crude question, don't you think?'

'I didn't realize until you said it. Maybe I shouldn't have asked so directly.'

Aryan was afraid he would upset her. He was hesitating before every word, and he knew she sensed him.

'I'm only teasing, yes. I write. I look at people, and I try to imagine what their dreams are like and write about them.'

Her hair was short. He could see it rustle like grass in the wind. It was almost as though the night was haunting him with her words, and it all seemed synchronized.

'That is interesting.'

'Do you think so?'

She looked across at him for the first time since they started their walk. Then she looked straight ahead.

'What if the people you look at are just a part of your dream, a much more elaborate plan? What if the dreams you imagine these people are having all belong to you? Maybe none of this is real.'

'Are you saying I am imagining you? That you are a fragment of my imagination?'

'Maybe.'

'Then I shall not complain.'

He felt his cheeks flushed. He could sense her smile, but he dare not look at her, might his sparkling eyes betray his pounding heart.

'If you were a part of my dream, you would be dressed differently though.'

'Do you not like the way I'm dressed?'

'It's too insignificant to be a part of my dream. I would have noticed otherwise.'

'Maybe your dream is focusing on my thoughts more than my appearance.'

'Then you must have clearer thoughts for my dreams to frame you better.'

'If I am your dream, shouldn't you give me better thoughts for me to speak to you, for me to be clearer?'

'No one is created. All dreams are merged like the dark universe. You have walked into my dream, and I into yours.'

Aryan felt strange. It seemed as though she was deriving thoughts he once believed in. Her words were opening up the conscious realm of his sleepless dwelling.

'You're cold. Your hands are trembling. Let's go back.'

He turned and followed her obediently; her feet left marks in the wet ground below them. He followed behind her for a while before catching up to her. She was walking with a brisk pace, her chin arched slightly upwards, the smile on her face unmoving, and he could almost feel her conversing with the moon.

They returned home. She gave him a warm hug and returned to her room. He stood right where he was. It seemed strange to him how easily the universe took and gave. Was it governed, or was he just another puppet on a string? Was she right? Was he truly a dream in her dream? His fingers were tingling. He turned and walked to his bed. It was a white bed; it seemed rather familiar. His walls were a different colour.

'It's time to sleep.'

13

The Unhappy Jester

' Fate and chaos,
  Eloquent in the sky,
Pale storms coursing through our veins,
Dwell upon mysteries,
Turgid and turbulent,
Dream of molten eyes,
Sorrows will pass,
Some will forget,
The birds will fly,
The trees will fall,
In the night, there is fire,
In the night, agony,
She's a mistress of desire,
Foresight of dread,
Living in patience,
Glancing at leaves,
The drifting breeze sweeps them away,
Dreams love and all.'

Cloaked in shadow, masked in darkness, and in haste, a hooded figure rode through pouring rain and windy skies. Peals of thunder cackled in the sky as darkness lost strength in flashing moments of purple hysteria in the moonless night.

Tendrils of mistlike smoke rose through his horse's flaring nostrils. She showed no signs of fatigue, her muscles reverberating like a breathing machine. She reflected the hooded figure's haste, one with thought and aligned in dream.

She galloped through muddy waters with graceful ease, gliding terrifically and fast. Her chest was heaving, contracting, and expanding in flashes of a midnight sky.

Haste burdened man and beast; cold black hands gripped on to the flowing mane, his legs warming the sides of his companion. He did not guide; she knew.

Nothing was visible of the hooded rider, and in flashes in the night, a black mask and dreamless eyes gleamed. Across his shoulder was slung a cylindrical object. It was speckled with the night's rain, moist and heavy. It betrayed no sign of importance, yet it was.

Arched against the wind and torrential rain, the figure looked straight into the black, never flinching. He saw what others couldn't perceive. He saw his destination, yet the moment was an illusion.

She was slender, her skin dark and her flowing mane black. She was one with the night, a dream united with chaos. Her eyes were glassy, yet the only star in the night sparkled in their darkness. As they surged forward, the cloaked figure glanced back into the night. He was anticipating the presence of a multitude of flaring nostrils pursuing him. For now, however, he was alone, and none but the steady and thunderous gallop accompanied him in the silent purple night.

There was burden on his mind,
lament in his soul,
a story to be told.
The darkness haunted him,
yet his gaze was steely,
If not for the star in her eye,
the fire on her brow,
all would be lost,
if not gone already.
They were being hunted by shadows in the dark,
invisible yet omnipresent pursuers,

thundering hooves, silent in the rain.

There was no morning light awaiting him or his galloping companion. Who he was, only time would tell. For now, he was just a shadow trying to betray time. He carried with him the scroll, and in the scroll was withheld the mystic tales of the colourful universe and her impending pathos.

Without the story, all would be truly lost, all finished. He was cloaked in shadow for time unknown now even to him. He wasn't always dark. He had transformed with the universe from colour to nothing. There was a time when he too was robed in colour and his companion white like snow with a beautiful golden mane.

Time and fate had betrayed them. Now they were cast in shadow and chaos. He had waited, abiding his time, solitude his lone companion, hoping once again for the cloak of darkness to be lifted so he could smile again. He was Lýpi, the last unhappy jester. All had thought him vanquished; all thought him gone, silent in the darkness that surrounded them.

Yet Lýpi waited and watched. Every moment, his strength was faltering, his faith meandering. Yet he stood on the edge of the darkness, staring into the void, hoping for a drop of blue into which he could sink and revive.

Now he had sensed it, and so had the darkness. They pursued him, for light must not be revived and dreams must be hollow.

He had been a captive to his own secrets, cloaking his subconscious, for his foe was strong and it was folly to fight when immortality had passed.

Lýpi, the lonely king, had chosen alone to fight against fortitude and not live in gratifying absolute of immortality. He chose chance as his fate, not destiny, for destiny is an illusion created by the universe to believe what is not.

He knew the answers to darkness and ego, yet he was too weak to stand against the might of a satiated realm. No words could awaken them, for the sponge was dripping with the anti.

'I am Lýpi, the illusionist. Mighty is my folly, and dark is the night.'

He was muttering under his breath. Yet it echoed in the void around him, loud and deep. His horse came to a halt, almost throwing him off. She had frozen. In front of her was a white mattress. Lýpi's hands were trembling.

'It cannot be.'

'It is.'

On the mattress lying in the muddy water was a clock and a radio.

'It is me Mikhail. Do you recognize me? Did you really think we would not find you?'

There was a silence as Lýpi stared at the two objects on the almost white mattress.

'Such a silly king. The sad king.'

Mikhail's voice boomed over the talking radio.

'Quiet, you fool! I do not want you to interfere.'

'Sorry, Mr Mikhail.'

'I really do not understand why this insolent fool is always with me. He serves me no purpose.'

There was a glassy gaze in Lýpi's eyes. He was afraid.

'You have been watching us, haven't you? But we have been watching you too, great messenger. Do you think they do not know? Do you think they weren't watching? There is no purpose you will succeed in fulfilling.'

Lýpi was smiling. He wasn't afraid. It was too late to be frightened; he only heard.

'When darkness has taken the universe and when the great king is vanquished, lost forever from memory and time, his dreams would wander, and his secrets would be discovered. The conscience would haunt him, and he would be lost in form and soul yet hidden, devoid even of being, one with the energy of the universe. A drop of blue in the black universe would bring back what was lost. The jester's last tale would awaken. The king would return once again to restore the lost story and bring colour to the universe. This is the prophecy, is it not?'

Lýpi's eyes were still glassy. He gazed at the mattress, restless yet not anticipating, for all thoughts were an echo and all dreams, audible.

'Well, this prophecy is rubbish, everyone knows it. The ones you seek are already gone. Forget your quest. Have a coffee.'

'Well said. Let's all have some coffee, shall we?'

'Why must you be such a pest?'

'Listen to me. I carry this burden, it is mine. The darkness knows, yet I will fight. I am no immortal, but my dreams still believe. I was once master of light. Without it, we are lost. Illusions and reality must be one again.'

'You are so silly. Can you take me with you? I really don't like this rain and the company of this annoying radio.'

'Now you must leave my dream, dear friend. I must make haste before it is too late.'

His horse lost her glassy gaze and jumped over the mattress. He dared not look back. Who knows what illusion might appear to haunt his visions?

'Take me with you. I am the mighty Mikhail.'

Mikhail's voice dissolved into the night sky, leaving only him and the heaving breath of his horse. As lightning cackled, reigniting his remorse, he saw in the flashes of light all around dead wasteland. Not a tree took breath in this darkness. There was no life. The air he breathed seemed lifeless. Was he even breathing?

He could feel the strain of his companion. Dreams were truly dying; the magic had passed. There were large masses of rock all around, sharp and jagged, gleaming in the moonlight like daggers. They seemed almost as if they had been polished.

'Diamonds in the sky, daggers all around, and no air to breathe. Seems about right.'

In the distance, he could see dark shadows move across his vision, drifting and gliding, shadows of once-greater beings now with arched backs and dark stature. The flashing light in the sky enhanced their silhouette, but only for a fraction, before throwing them back into the plague they were so accustomed to.

He rode. His horse was slowing down, not afraid but exhausted. She sensed the end of her journey, her last journey. He sensed her; she sensed him. In unity they moved, their last journey as one. Great decaying structures mounted high on rocks surrounded him. The once-great city of Skepsi now lay in ruin. Her tall regal dreams were now hunched across moss-laden floors, waiting for inevitable fate. The once-grand colonnades supporting great halls with mighty light and bright eyes now did not even dare to dream of olden days.

'In Skepsi there will always be hope,
In Skepsi there will be dream,
Darkest moments, brightest nights,
Light, fiery light, flickering and burning bright,

In cold,
Sorrow and smile,
In Skepsi there will always be light.
I dreamt of cities with breath,
I dreamt of cities with soul,
In Skepsi my dreams came true.
Beautiful and bright her smile,
Deep and blue her eyes,
A city with life,
In the darkest night,
In the coldest eyes,
I knew,
In Skepsi there will be light.'

Lýpi's voice resonated through the towering daggers around him. It was full of angst, bright with fading hope.

Masked figures, cloaked and hunched, appeared form behind the decaying colonnades. Perched on top of them were wicked-looking birds, dark with bead-black eyes.

The high steps to the city seemed almost to shiver upon Lýpi's words. The immortals of the city had been awoken from a stupor, just momentarily in the immeasurable passing of time.

They felt his words. It reignited a flame within their icy-cold insides, yet it had already begun to fade. A figure approached the edge of the steps and looked down upon Lýpi. He did not slump, he did not flinch, and he looked down at Lýpi, no remorse no fear.

'These words have not been echoed in our halls for infinity. You are not welcome here, mortal jester king. This is no longer the great city of Skepsi. Now we are slaves of darkness. We have no king, we have no dream, and the wait has been too long. Now there is only sleepless slumber here. You will not find what you have come to seek, nor is there an answer you will receive.'

Lýpi jumped off his horse. He had a smile on his face; his warmth almost seemed to bring light in the darkness.

'Ahh, the mighty immortals of the doomed city of Skepsi,
The mighty abandoned to live out their own plague
Until the very universe would envelop herself in death.

The mighty with no dreams
The purposeless immortals,
Living carcasses, with a lost story,
The masked immortals of Skepsi.'

There was a hollow silence as his words enveloped their absent minds.

'Do you come only to mock, or do you have a purpose?'

'I did not say I came here to seek or receive, and to me, it does not seem like you have much to do anyway.'

Lýpi was gazing into the hollow sockets that once contained fiery magic of the very universe.

'There is no reason to smile,
There is no reason to look into my eyes,
You will be lost,
The abyss is deep,
And the abyss is all.'

His voice was growing louder. It seemed almost as if Lýpi's words were awakening some sort of emotion in a morbid dream plagued with absence.

'I see you still possess your beautiful verses, a little rusty but good. Reminds me of days when I was a young boy sitting on the steps you now reject. Your words mesmerize my thought, great master of lost times.'

Lýpi almost believed he saw a flashing light in his master's eyes. The slumped hooded figures seemed to rise and move closer to him. His old master flicked his wrist, sending them back into their nightmarish stupor.

'I am impatient. Tell me what I already know.'

Lýpi sauntered closer to the steps. He only whispered, but his words were clear.

'Do you remember the stars in the night, the bright specks high above us? You once told me they were dreams, gleaming in the night. When we woke up, our dreams died, and the stars disappeared. I never woke up, so why did you?'

He took a deep breath; the wind was howling now. It was growing colder. The winds were moving; strangers approached.

'Do you see around me these slumped figures?
They were once great men,
Creators of the universe,

I was their king,
I led them to this darkness,
I betrayed them,
Here they lie now, hollow.
I alone have thought
My punishment is to think alone in this darkness
As these immortals with no mind sit empty.
Now I must suffer with them.'

Lýpi felt no angst in his old master's voice; it made him wonder how dark the plague truly was. His face was flinching.

'No fate is sealed,
No story is lost,
I have it with me,
We still have time in this fragmented universe,
All is not lost.'

'This night is a frightening place to be in, is it not?'

Lýpi felt a shiver run down his spine; his words froze him from within. They haunted him.

'Do you remember the clear blue universe when there was no darkness, only dreams and chaos? When our story echoed like poetry through flowing meadows of green and yellow? Do you remember the dragons in the sky, truth in our eyes, and warmth in the earth?'

His master looked at him unmoved.

'It was all a lie, wasn't it?'

Lýpi had to go on; he knew there was no other way.

'It was, yet it is better than this truth. Let us go back to sleep and dream of bright days.'

'Remember . . .'

A vision passed before Lýpi.

'He was just a small boy. He wore a uniform, grey shorts and a white T-shirt. He was standing, staring at the sky. It was the first time he had looked up and couldn't see the sun. The air around him pricked his skin. He was trembling but could not understand why. He had never felt fear. He could see ahead in the distance his master and his followers behind standing dressed in their usual white, looking into the sky. He did not find this strange even though he had never seen them like this. Their arms were stretched out. One by one, he saw his elders step off the cliff. Without knowing, he knew what was happening. As they walked off the cliff, with arms extended out birdlike, their robes turned to night, their eyes beady black. The sky darkened in an instant; the sun disappeared. They looked towards him. "Come," they said, but he stood erect, unflinching, a little boy gazing into the very heart of darkness. He was pure—he would always be.'

Lýpi was trembling; he had long abandoned this memory. The story had been abandoned; ego had taken the great men, leaving behind only Lýpi, the jester prince and now king. He knew they would come for him, so he disappeared with the last story into chaos. They called him the mad hatter, the last jester king of Skepsi. Why his elders chose the path of negated philosophy and enslaved dreams was simple to his innocent mind. They thought of the end, no matter how mighty a mind. No dreams, nothing more.

This is frightening; the mind negates the notion of absolute darkness, very similar to how the universe did not swallow itself into non-existence once darkness had overwhelmed the very purpose of her existence.

His master felt Lýpi's thoughts; they were reverberating in the open night that gleamed over once-mighty halls and faces. His voice was as cold as the chill that ran down Lýpi's spine.

'Yes, for what is the universe if not our very conscience, the perceivable reality of the infinite illusion?'

'I knew you were tempted by ego and immortality. I knew darkness and the end frightened you. At what cost?'

'The masked immortals, creators of the universe, were truly cursed by their very own greed and ego. For time passed us by. Trees withered away, but we stood tall against the thundering probabilities of universal epoch and faced immortality with stern faces and rigid hearts. Nothing is final, not even destiny. One by one, as the immortals aged like all creatures of the sun and moon, their minds withered away, leaving behind only unending life. Desires and emotions vanished, for the mind grew weary of thoughts and changes. All was gone, leaving behind only the jester and his timeless plague. In our immortality lay our greatest treasure. Yet in this gleaming paradise was our mightiest folly. It crumbled the mighty race of thinkers into hollow, voiceless memories, waiting for the end of the universe. The time of hope and revival, like dawn, had passed. Now all that remained was an insatiable desire for the end, the true and final demise of the universe.'

'All souls are bent to universal energy. Mine is still alive. There is hope to revive yours.'

'Lýpi, you already know our souls have withered away. Nothing remains of us but a thought and a word. Your soul bears the lost story. It contains the power to awaken the dark slumber, but sadly, Lýpi, all is dead, all has passed.'

'I do not believe in the soul master. I do not believe the fate of the universe belongs only to one philosophy. We are the story, not just our soul. You can be awoken, master.'

'Do not beg, Lýpi. Your arrival has been in vain. You should have remained where you were and let your days pass you by, for you chose the path of light, and here where you stand, it will only pass.'

Lýpi looked straight into the black hollow pockets that belonged to what was once his master. He spoke slowly, mocking with a gentle smile on his face.

'Light is meant to fade, is it not? With my dawn, there shall also be dark, a dark I am not afraid to partake, for there is where we all belong, possessors of the mortal life force.'

There was a voice in the cold, chill air. It boomed over the plains. 'Welcome, king of immortals, long have we awaited your arrival.'

As the voice passed, Lýpi's companion staggered, pained by the darkness. He looked towards her, warmth in his eyes.

'Do not let voices in the sky frighten you. There will always be light within you and me.'

'Not forever. You have held the story for long enough. Now it is time for it to truly end.'

Lýpi looked towards his old master; he was slumped back into darkness with his companions. He was truly lost.

'Do you really believe I carry this fable, this myth? Do you really believe I am the chosen one to revive the lost light?'

'The universe is not yet lost. The immortals govern a paradigm of darkness, but we sense the presence of dawn.'

Lýpi continued smiling; a warm breeze stirred around him. His master, slouched in the darkness, realized the truth. The darkness was sucking the life out of Lýpi. He was on his knees now.

'You knew they were coming.'

'They were never gone.'

There was a loud thud. Lýpi turned around; his companion lay in the mud behind him, heaving her last breath. Her journey was over. Lýpi turned back towards his master. He gazed with empty eyes at him.

'You are an immortal too! You lied about the story. You do not possess it, yet now we know it exists. Now we know there is hope.'

'There was always hope, master, now I can pass.'

Lýpi collapsed in the mud. A bright light flashed in the sky. It was warm like the sun.

14

Revival

It was quite a chilly afternoon; he was to meet Mila at the park. She would be sitting under the tree, reading a book. He was worried he wouldn't recognize her. It all felt like a dream to him, all a drifting breeze of illusion and reality. He sat upright on his bed and observed the room he waited with so much anticipation in. It had a crisp mahogany door; it almost felt alive, and it was chipping from the bottom. As the door ended, the floor began. It was covered in a pinstriped rug, red, and beige.

Above the carpet ran a runner the colour of the mahogany door. The walls were covered in wallpaper that would grace the living rooms of a bourgeoisie Parisian apartment on the Seine. The room was graced by a single white fixed French window. It was elevated from the bottom and had a regal height. The view outside was not of the Seine. It was of a narrow street with apartment buildings not more than four storeys tall. The structure looked old. Her bricks had mould, yet it looked graceful.

At short intervals were located similar single fixed white French windows. All the windows opened into tiny balconies, which were accompanied by ornate wrought-iron grills and tiny flowerpots. A few balconies were graced by a chair and their lonely smoking companions.

Aryan was anxious; he was to see her again. His mind was blank. He did not know what he would say, and he did not know how she felt. He got out of bed and dressed up. Aryan wondered when she had left. Had she even slept? He had found a note near his bed: 'Meet me at the park when you're awake. I'll be under the tree. I'll find you. Love, Mila.'

He was rather confused, for the park had many trees and under these trees sat a lot of faces. Aryan put on a dark-blue jacket, under which he wore a white crumpled T-shirt he had slept in. He stepped out of his room and into the street. He was greeted by a gleaming sun and a cold breeze. The park wasn't far away, yet it seemed longer than natural. He was nervous. He felt queasy within, yet he knew the moment he laid eyes upon her all would pass. Aryan saw the park across the street. It was lush and green, and faces sat on benches reading books; others were under spreading trees, holding hands.

'So many lives, so similar. Yet every mind a dream, different from another.'

He crossed the street; it was empty, only a few fallen leaves drifted along seemingly unaware of the morbidity of life. Music from the distance penetrated his thoughts. The words were blurry and in a strange language. The garden had a winding brick path with well-groomed grass on either side. Miniature lamp posts, about a foot high, highlighted the winding brick pathway. They were black and had frosted glass illuminating the grass below. Pigeons wandered the grassy pastures for pieces of grain and bread, remained of lost conversations under the sun. Aryan walked a little ahead and stood looking around. He could sense her, and he knew she was watching him.

Then he saw her, sprawled gracefully on her back, looking into the skies, her eyes closed. She wore a thick black overcoat and a red blouse underneath. The bright red made her already pale skin look further cold. Her lips were red; her eyes, lined with jet-black mascara. She heard his feet rustle through the grass and opened her eyes. She gave him a warm lonely smile; he could almost feel pity in it. She had a diary next to her; it was open, and the pages shifted position in the gentle breeze. She saw him looking at it.

'I knew you would find me.'

'What if I hadn't?'

She laughed and picked up her diary.

'Little birds took to the sky,

Their wings glistened and gleamed,

Tiny drops of rain,
Falling from above,
Their beaks moist,
Ruffled feathers,
Rainy pleasures.'

Aryan was looking at her intently; she was not her usual self. Her words weren't intense; he was almost not anxious.

'Since we tend to have rather morbid conversations, I decided to lighten up the already bright afternoon by sharing my love for the tiny drops of rain and little birds flying in the summer sky.'

'Sometimes I feel like you can read my mind.'

He was sitting next to her with his legs crossed; she had rolled over on her stomach, her feet in the air moving to and fro. She had taken her shoes off; her feet had chipped red nail paint on it.

'That Aryan is because I can!'

Aryan smiled as she stretched, letting her body into complete ease. She turned her head sideways, the grass caressing her face, and looked at Aryan. Every time he looked into her blue eyes, he could see his reflection; he could read his own emotion.

'Let's read clouds.'

She turned on to her back and rested her head in her pale white palms. Aryan followed lying on his back and looking up into the sky. He glanced at her just to make sure she was looking up too. Mila was pointing her hand into the sky, trying to touch it.

'I've always wanted to fly into the sky, sit in the clouds, and look at the faces below. I wonder how the imaginary gods feel. Do they wish to come down where we are and look up?'

Aryan felt a sense of déjà vu. Her words seemed familiar. He knew, yet his mind would not disclose.

'Look up and tell me what you see.'

Aryan was nervous. He didn't want to sounds meagre. Yet his mind, as he looked into the clouds, couldn't muster the courage to create words that would generate thought in her mind. He could see, yet he felt tense. Mila could sense his angst. She turned her head towards him, a silvery laughter escaped her.

'I'll go first.'

Aryan was glad. She held his hand and pointed into the sky with her finger. She was drawing a shape, her finger and his.

'See that there? That's the snout and the two little clouds are the puffs of smoke.' She moved their hand lower. 'That is her neck with the scales on it, and lower, the big cloud is her belly, full of all the dreams she's swallowed, and right at the back, there is her tiny stubby tail, a rather fat dragon with a tiny tail.' Mila was giggling. She turned towards him. 'Do you see it?'

He couldn't, but he didn't have the strength to tell her.

'Umm, yes, I see her.'

'Such a liar. I made that up! Look at that cloud. It's completely round.' She was laughing. 'You do this to make me feel happy? You really shouldn't. Now take my finger and show me what you see.'

Aryan held her hand and looked in the sky. He wanted nothing more. A voice echoed in his head, 'Blink, boy, just you blink. He's coming for you.'

Aryan looked up. He couldn't move. The skies went black, and there were flames. Trees around him were on fire. Mila lay next to him, unconscious. He couldn't breathe. A red sun gleamed straight at him, and then there was a shadow. An ear-piercing howl shredded the skies. A dragon appeared in the skies. Her body was elegant, and her scales black and unreflective. It seemed to have absorbed all the light around, sucked the life of all living. Only Aryan lay frozen, gazing into her slanting milky white eyes.

She looked ragged, her wings running full of sinewy veins from her shoulders to her long slender tail. From her silted nostrils rose tendrils of dark smoke. A hooded figure rode atop her, covered in black. Only two gleaming eyes shone, red like the sun beyond. A long tongue curled around her mouth, exposing gleaming sharp teeth. She was suspended in mid-air. Only her wings moved, gently keeping them afloat. The hooded figure jumped off her back and landed nimbly on his feet.

The grass shivered slightly, almost parting for him. His dragon was high above; this wasn't an ordinary man. He unsheathed a blade from under the robes. It was silver, her edges catching hues of the red sun, magical and surreal, reflecting his dragon's steely claws, gleaming for death.

'The day has passed,

The grass has dried.

We return now,
Master of the skies.
Long ago, we abandoned truth,
Now this is where we dwell,
Dragon, cloak, and night.
Unsheathed sword,
Breathing fire,
We have come,
We have come to take what we lost,
For now it is time to rise,
Light to dark.'

Aryan looked towards Mila. She was all he cared about, and she was still unconscious. She was hovering in the air next to him, her arms dangling loose. He back was arched slightly backwards, her face looking towards the dragon. It seemed like she was moving towards them. Aryan tried moving towards her. He wanted to hold her. A loud fearful thunder filled the air. The hooded man in front of him was speaking, yet his lips did not move. He was mocking Aryan, laughing at his misery.

'The dragon growled,
The dragon roared,
All mighty kneeled before,
We will take her,
For her time has come,
You shall be spent,
No lost dreams,
Only darkness.'

The hooded man walked towards Aryan. He was tall, towering over him.

'Why is everyone always towering over me?'

'That, boy, is because you are insignificant.
To the city we take her,
For she is the keeper,
To the city we take her,
For without her,
There is no dream.'

The dragon shot a red fiery flame out of his mouth full of jagged spikes, lighting the grass around Aryan on fire.

'I will fight.'

His legs were trembling; his body, numb. There was a deep laugh as the hooded figure raised his gleaming sword in the end.

'You are not worthy, boy.'

Mila's eyes opened; she was still suspended in mid-air. She turned her head towards Aryan.

'He is here for me. I must go now.'

Her voice caressed his will. The dragon in the sky bowed her head down and made a hollow moan. The hooded man stared at his dragon and, with a slight motion of his hand, turned her head up. She roared; she was in pain. She was not his companion; she was his slave.

'Do not stay up, I will go.

Someday we will meet, in this dream or the next.

Remember me, for I will remember you.

Remember my voice, remember my smile,

For I will wait for you.

Remember, Aryan.'

She looked back ahead; her voice was weak. The grass below her milky-white feet began to grow longer. They wrapped themselves around her. Mila's body drifted towards the dragon. She held Mila with her steely claws. The hooded figure turned around and, with his sword, sliced the grass; they floated in the air for a moment before being carried away in the sultry breeze. What was happening?

'I will ask you a riddle. Only if you answer will I let her go.'

'And what if I fail?'

'*I will burn your soul.*

There was once a mighty king,

There was once a dark raven,

There was once a crazy clown,

They all lived in a mystic town,

The clock spoke,

Yet no time it ever told.

In a room they sat,

Where colours changed.
Sometimes he flew,
And then he slept.
Whom do I speak of?'
Aryan was confused. He did not understand a word of what was said.
'This makes no sense. Can you repeat it?'
'To humour myself, I shall.'
Aryan tried to focus; he had to save Mila.
'There was once a petty boy,
There was once a lazy bird,
There was once a glorious prince,
They all slept in a dreamless town,
The radio spoke,
On a floor they sat,
Where textures changed,
Sometimes he flew,
Then he slept.
Whom do I speak of?'
'This is completely different from what you said earlier.'
'And yet the same.'
'This really is not fair.'
'You dare speak to me that way.'
Aryan hesitated; he couldn't think. No thought passed his empty mind; he was going to lose her.
'I have not all day to wait for you. Tick-tock.'
'Is it a pigeon?'
'Of course not! Now you shall pass.'
Aryan closed his eyes. So this was how it was to end. He glanced at Mila one last time. One last time, he smiled. The hooded figure unsheathed his sword. It glistened red and bright, and in a single moment, he plunged it into Aryan's heart. Aryan awoke with a jolt; it was a dream.

His chest was throbbing; his brow was covered in sweat. His throat was parched, yet he sat in his room, on his bed. There was no dragon, nor was there a sword. Aryan was relieved, not because he could still breathe, but because Mila still remained. The thought of her gone devastated him.

It seemed less of a nightmare, for on her leaving, he had passed. To wait would be a nightmare, to hope for infinity that one day she would return. His chest still hurt. He looked down, and he could see a bloodstain.

Aryan ignored it; it was still dark outside. He could hear the drops of rain against his window. The moonlight vaguely illuminated his floor. It seemed as though he was yet to wake from a dream. He wondered who the hooded creature was and why the dragon obeyed his command.

What dream was this that led to reality? What illusion was this where he bled? As he gazed out of the window, he could swear he saw a dark-winged beast fly into the distant night. It couldn't be. He wanted to see if Mila was still asleep. He wanted to hold her in his arms and never let go. Her warmth would satiate him into dreamy slumber. Sadly, he knew the universe was not so kind. He knew that in a momentary lapse of time, she would be gone; so would he.

A pigeon sat on the ledge outside; it had a keen gaze, staring at him as if perceiving his thought. Dragons of the sky, thought Aryan. The mighty pigeon and the lonely jester, guardians of the universe, now slaves of darkness. He closed his eyes and fell asleep.

'Not so easily will they let you pass,
Never will there be calm,
The darkness and light have taken all.
You may choose, but chaos befalls all.
Do you believe your journey is so easy?
Do you believe darkness is welcoming?
The masters sat in mountains,
The masters prayed for sanctity and light.
They all went crazy,
They all went wild.
On their bodies grew trees,
Their souls turned to dragons,
Some dark, some bright.
Burning mountains through the night,
One by one, they fell,
Some to fate, yet none to grace.
What tragedy befell them, no one could tell,

For all had passed,
Hollow cries and empty laughter.
Then came the riders,
They captivated their minds,
Turning to darkness, the dragons truly fell.
Remember, all great beings felt tragedy.
All is yet to be lost.'

15

The Loathing Sun

A single sparrow sat on Aryan's window, sill chirping a loud clanking melody. The notes were distant and clear disturbed only by her feathers ruffling in the chilly air.

The window had dewdrops on it, symbolic to the bright sun high up in the sky. A lone shadow of a leafless tree graced the porch outside his window. The raw branches gave it a scarecrow like appearance. It seemed almost grotesque. There was a sharp trill; her song was over. His eyes awakened to a pleasant summer morning.

Dreams can be quite vague. His brow was covered in sweat, and his hands were trembling slightly. It was as if he hadn't slept at all. He tried conversing with the sparrow, but she flew away. The last time he had spoken to a sparrow, it had collapsed on the floor and died.

Aryan had blamed the chill weather for the occurrence, but all the other sparrows knew his words had curdled their sparrow friend's heart to an absolute halt. They had decided to keep their distance. The absence of their company had saddened him quite a bit, for he had quite a soft spot for them.

A long ray of dusty yellow light crept through the gap in his blinds, illuminating his wooden floor. Tiny particles floated in the illuminated patch. It was surreal. As time passed, the light gradually crept further forward and settled on Aryan's outstretched foot. Aryan loved sunlight, especially on a cold summer morning. It made him feel special and almost made him forget his ordeal with the sparrows. He felt as though it was a gesture of comfort and warmth by the sun in these unfortunate days when sparrows died because of the cold. Aryan turned to his side table and stretched his arm out. He turned the dial of the radio. It had a chagrin cover, a 1935 Soviet model made to counter the more expensive ones. This seemed vaguely familiar.

It was time for his favourite talk show. They were going to talk about the sun and the universe and other such frivolous things with some highly learned person. He claimed to have mastered the understanding of the universe and her benefactors. There was a white noise; the programme had already begun.

'The sun really does try hard. So much dedication to remain in one single place and burn, no matter what dimension my mind wanders. The blistering sun persists to be blistering and hot.'

He would have loved to have this conversation with the sparrows, but for now, he would have to listen to some strangers have it.

'The colour does change occasionally to a deep pink or a leaf green, but it does keep burning.'

Aryan did not realize this deep-set understanding for the sun, probably floating around somewhere in his chaotic and depressed subconscious, a singular positive in an infinite of negative.

'You are a distant relative of the sun. The sun hates you though. There is no denying that fact.'

'Why would the sun hate me?'

The interviewer sounded intrigued, but it was a facade. He couldn't care less. He repeated the same exaggerated phrases day in and day out. Even with his emotions, he sounded robotic, but not to his listeners. They loved him.

The person being interviewed at the other end had a calm singular voice. It did not show any hesitation. His replies were clean. Most of the persons being interviewed every week seemed calm and stable. It was almost as though they had been asked to be an alter ego to the interviewers exaggerated awe and excitement.

'The sun detests being so hot all the time. It's not very pleasurable as you so calmly assume. The sun spends most of his time trying to blow up the silly planet with its silly people. The sun has an immense amount of free time and absolute lack of company. This would make anyone bitter.

'The sun has an inferiority complex known only to him, unlike the likes of you who truly considered him mighty and rather warm. This infuriates him to no extent, hence his unending attempts at blowing things up.

'The moon he ignores, well because the moon was the moon and probably made of cheese. There is no fun in melting cheese. I personally love melting cheese, but I doubt the sun has any interest.

'The sun, apart from focusing on exploding you, me, and his fellow earthlings, also wants to explode anything in his proximity, thus generating a rather large amount of angst in his neighbouring celestial friends.

'We always misinterpret the sun's warmth to be his way of acknowledging his presence in this cold lonely universe. This, however, is a great misunderstanding for the sun despises the universe and all that are part of this illusion.

'Never call the universe an illusion. Nothing annoys her more. The earth, the totality of it, to the sun philosophically and literally is like an annoying piece of food particle stuck in a precariously unreachable portion of one's mouth where, no matter how much you tried reaching with your tongue, it just wouldn't get dislodged.

'To imagine having this feeling for an eternity is not very appealing. The only way to get rid of this feeling would require a toothpick, hence the need for a gigantic toothpick being one of the sun's major demands to the universe.

'What further agitates the sun is the universe not providing him with a giant toothpick to dislodge earth and her silly inhabitants, you being one of them. The universe being the universe is quite aware of the unhappy nature of the sun and his rather extravagant demands.

'Now the universe, creator and destroyer of every singular, and these singulars being somewhere close to the proximity of infinite, finds it difficult to offer karmic retribution to every minor injustice.

'It takes time getting around, even for the universe. The universe, on multiple occasions, has tried for the sun to realize through subtle messages that it would be extremely difficult to provide him with a giant toothpick to dislodge the earth.

'The universe has tried to imbibe a philosophy of "burn and let live" in the sun's demented philosophy but has clearly failed to do so.'

'Has the sun ever been provided by any form of retribution in the past?'

There was not a hint of sarcasm in the interviewer's voice. Aryan was captivated; he moved his leg out of the sun.

'The sun annoyed the universe to unending extents but, in her attempts to satisfy the sun's desires, had decided to provide him with some form of retribution. The sun had been given freedom to blow up multiple large floating rocks in space, giving him great joy. The angst of these rocks a second prior to being vaporized was quite significant. However, luckily for the universe, the sun was quite efficient with these tasks of annihilation and had vaporized them before their lack of karmic justice reached the sore ears of the universe. The sun, however, was never truly satisfied, making the universe abandon him for the moment.'

'It is said that the universe does let the sun blow the earth up in the future.'

'This is assumed to be true, for the populous of the earth gets way to demanding, their output towards universal contribution is nothing if not negative. Sometimes even the universe loses its patience, especially since a gigantic ball of fire is already pestering her to be provided with a giant toothpick. The universe, agreed, is very giving, but some demands are just too much to comply with. Now the universe could have provided the sun with this toothpick, but then the creativity of demands would far exceed her patience. So she lets the sun blow earth up in the future.'

'What opinion does the universe have of being considered an illusion?'

'This is one of the prime reasons she lets us get erased from her dark and meaningless existence. It annoyed the universe to no extent, being called an illusion. After aeons of karmic retribution and other such activities, being called an illusion would upset anyone.

'Now picture this. My friend really liked blue shoes but didn't have any. He asked the universe, and she provided even though she could make no sense of the requirement of shoes in the first place. To get my friend these shoes, she had to pull a lot of strings in eddies of universal retribution. A lot of paperwork!

'However, these senseless demands never stop. Eventually, the universe gets frustrated with man and his notion of what she is philosophically and literally. So the sun gets to blow all of us up. This, however, doesn't stop the sun from having more demands. So the sun gets wiped out too. This friend is the reason nothing lasts in the continuum of universal time. Too many unnecessary demands!'

Aryan loved listening to this programme. He found it very intriguing. Currently, he sat in bed, laughing at the absurdity of this discussion. It felt unreal yet perfect for his morning entertainment. Initially, he had decided to pay attention and not judge, but he really couldn't help himself. He still kept his leg away from the sun.

As his mind wandered away from the words emanating from the vintage radio, he heard a scuffle of feet outside his door. No one really ever came to visit him, yet there were one or multiple persons outside his door. This did not surprise him. Some company would do him good. He got out of bed and walked towards the door. The floor below his feet creaked as he walked across the wooden rafters.

They were darkened with moisture now, giving his room the appearance of a space straight out some vintage story. The sounds outside came to a halt. They had heard the shuffle of his feet and had gone quiet. Just next to the door lay his shoes, which he put on without untying the laces.

He turned the doorknob, his head bent towards his feet. As the door opened, he saw in front of him two clowns. They did not seem very happy.

'Hello, would you mind closing the door and opening it in the next few minutes? It isn't time yet for us to meet you.'

Aryan obeyed. It all seemed normal to him. Not once did it bother him that two clowns, and not very happy ones, stood outside his door. After a few moments, he heard a knock on his door, and he opened. The two clowns stood in front of him. They wore ankle-length khaki pants, very loose and ragged. They were the jumper kinds, with grey stripes.

Beneath they wore white tattered vests. Their faces were covered in white powder, and their smiles turned upside down. Their noses were large and red.

'Hello.'

'Good morning.'

'Good morning.'

'We come bearing a message, Aryan.'

'We come bearing a message, Aryan.'

They both looked at each other and in sync like their words and put their fingers to their lips as if too tell each other to be silent. After a few moments of silence, Aryan realized they wore strange shoes. They were Oxfords but much too big for their feet and rather overworked.

They both carried bags with them, slung across their shoulders. Each wore a white glove one in his left and one in his right, so it would seem to an observer that they were a mirror image of each other.

'This message is of grave importance.'

'This message is of grave unimportance.'

'Perfect, just the kind I like.'

'They are your dreams.'

'They are your dreams.'

'Well, which ones?'

'We wouldn't know, sir.'

'We wouldn't know, sir.'

'I can see that the letters are opened.'

'So are your dreams!'

'So are your dreams!'

'Do you like my shoes.'

'When in doubt, look around,

When in doubt look around.

Wings and clouds,

Wings and clouds,

Brighter than the bluest blue,

Brighter than the bluest blue,

His shoes,

His shoes,

Lovely turquoise blue,

Lovely turquoise blue.'

'Well, they aren't exactly turquoise blue.'

Aryan took the letter from the outstretched hand of the clown. He looked at them. Their eyes were morbid, lonely, and lost. He recognized the envelope but couldn't recall from where. Aryan pulled the letter out.

'Will you wait for me?

I can't promise that,

Time changes people, remember?

Strangers with memories.'

There was more. Aryan dropped the letter. The clowns looked at him.

'We both have to follow our roads. Life is long, and dreams are scarce. Love, M.'

It wasn't their voice any more. It was a voice he could never forget.

16

The Fall

There was a loud screeching noise. Aryan awoke with a jolt.
'So you thought you would never return, did you?'
He couldn't recollect where he was. His mind kept sending him flashes of places he had been, but the scenario around did not match.

'You're back where you belong, boy. You're home.'

It was Mikhail's voice.

'Fate is strange, is it not?
It takes you on journeys,
Magical and quaint.
Then one day,
A storm comes, and clouds fade,
The sun is mute, and all is dream.
You see the grey,
The grey sees you,
Do you dare look?
Do you dare speak?
There is nothing,
Yet you have lost everything,
For back you come,
Beginning and end.'

As Aryan had anticipated, this negativity was graced by the celebratory voice that belonged to Lokhvitsky. He felt almost as though he had never left.

'Bravo! That was perfect.'

This was chaos to Aryan. There were voices all around, overbearing and loud. His head was throbbing.

'Coffee . . .'

'The boy gets to meet the jester king, and all he can think of is coffee.'

'Silence, I am master of this realm. Do not speak unless I command.'

As he turned his head upwards from the white mattress he lay on, he noticed he had returned to his room. There was only one difference. It seemed to have been cleaned. There were no feathers on the cold floor, nor was there colour on the walls. His environment was stark. There was a cup of coffee on the side table. This time, however, no mist rose from it.

A letter lay next to the cup, and a cigarette, its fire slowly fading out. Aryan was staring at the table; this was unnatural. Someone had been in his room, spent time. He was afraid; this was a sudden outburst of emotion.

He never felt any sense of emotion, especially not here. His hands were trembling, and his breathing was heavy. Aryan jumped out of bed, but his legs gave way.

'It's been longer than you imagine. Time has passed, yet the breeze is warm. Do not be scared, friend. Only a meandering smile sat beside you while you dreamt of dark and light.'

Aryan lay hunched on the floor. It was cold, like ice. He had landed on his bare knees and elbows, and he remained in that stance. His eyes focused on the floor.

'Your dreams have changed you. What purpose will this change serve?'

Aryan's head was ringing with this voice. He had no control over it.

'You are letting emotion dominate your reality. For none is real, you have only me and this cold floor.'

'Us, us.'

Lokhvitsky's mocking voice followed.

'Yes, and unfortunately, the clock and watch. I really don't understand what her need was to put them here.'

'Quiet, you talk too much.'

Aryan's eyes lit up.

'Who are you talking about? Who put them here?'

'It's nothing, dear friend. Sometimes even our words are transient and plagued with illness.'

'I thought you disliked Mikhail and Lokhvitsky?'

'You were gone for so long, I needed company.'

Aryan couldn't care less. His mind was spinning. It felt almost as if they were trying to get his mind disillusioned from the thought trying to make its way into his memory. He couldn't reach it.

'Do you know of the inverted city of dreams, beautiful carved colonnades, tall orders, and great minds? There was once a dreamer who graced the grand halls of this city. She dreamt of magic and hope. With her thought, the city grew, majestic and large. The cobbled roads leading to the city spoke of destiny, they spoke of desires. Yes, the inverted city of dreams.

'Mighty men with empty minds made their way to this great city, all who entered never returned. Cities they left behind for this destiny turned to dust, abandoned, hopeless. The inverted city grew, but all men outside couldn't look beyond her tall grey walls.

'Only tales were told of this city. One day a little boy stood at the edge of the cliff. Looking at these grand gates, he too dreamt of entering the city of dreams. He knew all were not permitted. He knew only the mighty were admitted. Yet mustering up his courage, he walked across the cobbled road and stood in front of the black gates. "What is it you want?" a beautiful voice caressed his mind. "I want entry into your city," he said. "There is nothing beyond these gates. You are still young. Do not return, for it is folly. The mighty abandoned their cities. Now the universe is dark." The boy turned and walked away.

'The gates opened. He turned around, and all he saw was darkness. Before the gates stood a girl, pale like the moon. Her light dress was flowing in the air. She smiled and spoke, "Only your dreams are real. Beyond these walls lie false hopes and lost smiles. I too dreamt once, I know you will return, not in this dream but another. Run now, you are still young." 'This was no inverted city of dreams, the dream snatcher.'

Aryan wasn't listening.

'Do you know who she was? Do you know who he was, boy?'

He did not know why the voice in his head spoke of the tale of the dream snatcher. It made no sense to him. He needed to return; he did not know where.

'Since he has awoken, he has changed.'

'He has become far too inquisitive.'

'This is all Lýpi's fault.'

'Do you truly believe he is the bearer of the story, which is just a fable?'

The voice in Aryan's head questioned with malice. Aryan was confused; he did not understand how voices spoke so casually of dreams and reality.

'How do you know about the jester king? How do you know all this!'

'Your dreams are visible to all you fools.'

Aryan was still on his elbows and knees. He slowly raised himself up, his back against the mattress, his knees on the cold floor. He looked towards the side table; the letter lay there, unmoved. His palms were covered in ink stain; he wondered where that had come from.

'You, my friend, are a storyteller, yet those stories you speak of abandoned you with tales incomplete.'

Lokhvitsky had gone weary with the intricate weaving of words.

'What a pointless story.'

'Lokhvitsky, you are too silly to understand.'

'I agree. I can never be like you, Mr Mikhail.'

'Now, Aryan, do you not think it was folly to abandon us like this? Do you not feel it was all a mistake? You must stay here now. We will ensure you dreams pass and you sleep silent.'

The voice in his head was coaxing him. I want to go back out. I must return to the light. There was a sparrow and kings; there were jesters and puppets. Aryan was restless. He knew he had been moved, for on the spongy white, there are no dreams, yet he had awoken with so much vision, his head resting on the grimy mattress.

'You were moved, boy, from stone to the white, for time was passing slow here but rapidly in dream. I, the mighty Mikhail, made sure of that myself.'

'What do you mean time is moving rapidly in dream?'

'Insolent fool, you do not realize the gravity of the situation, do you? This is not a one-dimensional universe as you so casually assume.'

'This makes no sense.'

'How dare you question my words, I am the mighty Mikhail.'

'I need to meet Urien. Maybe he will have answers.'

'Don't you remember? He is the one who sent you back. This is home, and there is no return now . . .'

Aryan was trembling. This could not be. He was to go on a journey; it could not be over, for it hadn't even begun.

'It seems like the jester king was wrong about you. Looks like you aren't the chosen one after all. What a pity.'

Everyone around was loathing; it diminished Aryan's tempted destiny. He was lost, listening in angst.

'The mad hatter, the silly mad hatter. I warned him. What a fool to believe he saw light in this hollow.'

There was a loud sound of laughter; a cackle thundered through the dark confines of his room. The walls were changing colour. They had gone grey. The coffee on the side table began to smoulder again. Dreams were stirring.

'It cannot be he has passed into darkness.' Mikhail's voice was trembling. There was complete silence. There were no visible openings, yet a cold breeze swirled around, eerie sounding, with lost prophecies of the night. It seemed all a rather too dramatic, but nonetheless necessary.

'The door is opened, dreams are awake.'

'In tearful mist,

Glancing eyes passed you by.

Closed eyes,

Dreaming of time.

Seasons passed,

Moons died,

Years passed.

Morbid nights,

No light.

Yet a voice,

Silvery and light,

Woke you up,

Sent you back.

Wait now,
Like you always did.
Nights will shine,
Never again,
Gleaming silver,
Cloudy skies,
A single drop,
Weeping eyes.'

Urien's voice echoed through his dark room.

'How is this possible? This is not your dimension, you must return.'

'I am Urien, captive to none, not even dreams.'

Aryan knew he recognized his voice. He was elated. A star sparkled in his eye; Urien was here to take him away dreams and all.

'You cannot enter here. It is forbidden. I am the master here.'

'You are Mikhail, are you not? I have heard about you. One more word, and you shall not have the capacity to speak again.'

'Can I speak?'

'Do you have anything to share with me Lokhvitsky?'

'Not really.'

'I thought as much.'

Aryan had a smile on his face; it felt strange. His face had not expressed such emotion in quite some time.

'As you might know, sporadic chaos has ensued. Minds are not what they once were. Jester's, pigeons, and clowns. We seem to be truly lost. What was once stable isn't any more. The mad jester king has passed, yet in the breeze, I can still feel him. All is not lost as you would love to believe, Mikhail. This is a fate you can accept but never make true.'

Urien was present, but there was no form; Aryan was confused. He could not relate to his words, yet he knew it was his way out.

'Dreams are passing from one realm to another. Time has travelled. Minds have passed. Listen to me, Aryan, you must pass through the door one last time. You must have the strength like you once did. This is not my place to take you. I am but a voice here, powerless yet existent. Goodbye, dear friend. Remember, magic nights, bright nights, the stars will shine. Gaze.'

Mikhail waited for Urien's voice to fade completely, and then with regained gusto, he spat. There were still tremors in his voice. 'Way out from where, boy, you will only be lost further. This is the abyss the universal abyss.'

In certain fleeting moments, I do believe we are monumental to the passing of time. As I sleep, do I truly dream. While I am awake, am I truly? These morbid thoughts plague me often, yet there is no recess. What door must I walk through? What is this light everyone talks of? Is there truly magic in the night? Gleaming stars to gaze at? Illusions are mighty. What is put forth before my eyes do not sparkle. Maybe I should fly. I have never looked up from where I stand, only the cold floor below me.

'Do not look up. This falsified enigma you have shall not last. Like the coffee on your table, it shall go cold. You will dry out. Do not look up. Do not gaze. Keep your eyes low. The magic will pass.'

'Why does everything I want to do bother you so much?'

'In haunting distance, obsolete words are being uttered. The premise is far more extensive than you can imagine. Do you ever see me look up?'

'Well, you are a box. You really couldn't look up even if you wanted to.'

Mikhail sensed tension in Aryan's voice. He could not let him leave again.

'Firstly, boy, that is unnecessarily offensive.'

'Great, just fantastic . . .'

'Quiet, Lokhvitsky, you fool. Secondly, we are not always trying to negate you from the positive. Do not derive conclusions from anticipated imaginations.'

'Such a silly boy . . .'

'Why must you always be an echo to his thoughts? Do you not have a mind of your own?'

The voices went silent. Ever since Aryan had woken up from his dreamy slumber, he had returned with a voice. He was questioning. His thoughts weren't obsolete any more. They couldn't be erased. The voices sensed the restless nature of his once-slothful mind. It frightened them to think he might leave their dimension once again never to return, for who wants to be forgotten, illusion or reality? The fear of becoming second to another dream, to slowly disappear into nothingness yet exist. It almost seemed to

Aryan as though he was controlling their thoughts the way they did his before his dream.

'Do you truly believe this? Do you truly believe you are now in control of us?'

The voice in his headed sounded rather sceptical.

'I did not think it out aloud.'

'Your dreams and thoughts are for all. They echo like drops of water falling into an empty vessel.'

Aryan was hesitating. He was frightened. His emotions were coming in the way of his dark clarity. This was a rare occurrence, and he did not enjoy it as much as he thought he would. His mind had begun to deceive him. Colours changed around him, and coffee got cold, yet he did not notice. His mind was drifting; his darkness, fading. His arms slowly stretched out, and his back arched backwards slightly. Aryan's eyes remained shut. He did not have the courage to open then and gaze upwards into the sky even though his body had propelled itself for that purpose.

'Keep them shut tight, boy. Do not fly. You will regret it.'

Aryan felt his hands disappear. The cold on his feet vanished, and he was floating. Aryan opened his eyes. All was dark around him, and above him was a black sky with sparkling stars. It was beautiful.

He felt warmth on his face, his mind lost thought. He went higher and higher. He wanted to touch the stars. He looked below. His room was a speck now, a little drop of light enveloped in a cloak of darkness. He could see his toes pointed downwards, his skinny legs trembling slightly.

Aryan looked back up, and with much gusto, he continued upwards. He was breaking free of all dreams. He would truly be free now.

He was stationary now, his body rotating slowly in the warmth. All around him, he saw glancing visions of lost thought. Was this where his memories lay hidden—high above him, in the labyrinth of stars?

A warm voice penetrated his mind. It was Mila's.

'Where you go, you will find me. Where I go, I shall not. My memory is fading, maybe I am waiting. The stars are shining, are they not? Yet the gleaming in your eye will be my brightest light. Do not dwell so far in my search. I am lost, so are you.'

Aryan's vision was blurred. His eyes had moistened, and he could feel tears roll down his face. He could not remember how she looked; all he knew was she was a dream he could relive forever. Her warmth flooded him; he felt in this moment how he did in her presence. Aryan could not see her, yet he could feel her soft hands caress against his, the fragrance from her hair brushing his face. Her laughter echoed in his hollow. His eyes were gazing at the stars; his mind, at her.

'Remember, Aryan, dreams and destiny.' Her voice faded into the night.

Had he escaped his prison? Could he drift like this forever, through dream and darkness? There was a loud peal of laughter; the night sky around him was vibrating, He was falling. Had wings had disappeared?

'Fly not too close to the sun,

Fly not too near the watery labyrinth they call the sea,

Icarus, follow me and only me.'

The laughter continued; Aryan accepted his fate. Death was better than the hollow he was enveloped in.

'Not so easily will I let you fall into the sea, boy.'

Aryan was flying upwards again; his wings were back. Was he truly free? Had they set him loose? He blinked, and as his eyes opened, he saw a surface above. The stars had vanished to be replaced by a single black layer of rigid morbid fear.

He was accelerating now; he was going to collide. He shut his eyes as he was about to crash into the wall of darkness, but he went straight through. It was like diving headfirst into a cold pool of water. As his eyes opened, a bright light blinded him; his feet felt cold again.

When the light cleared, he saw. Aryan was back in his room. His feet on the cold floor, feathers all around. Was there no way out?

'I told the boy not to fly,

Fools in the sky,

Gleaming stars called him back,

I told the boy the sea was old,

Like a dream,

Full of terror,

Dark and cold.'

Aryan fell to the floor; an unceremonious cackle greeted the thud his body made as it crashed against the cold, dark floor below.

'I warned you, boy, this is home. You must accept your fate. There is no journey. There is no impending fate.'

Aryan was drowsy. He knew what he had seen was no illusion; he knew the voices had not perceived his realities for him.

'She is nothing but illusion. We saw what you heard. We felt what you didn't, and dreams are passing. Yes, dreams and all.'

'I was falling. Why stop me? It was over. Why need me? Let me go.'

'You speak like a captive.'

'I feel like one.'

'This is your mind. Who is truly slave and who is master is a matter of interpretation.'

Mikhail interrupted rudely. He seemed annoyed more than usual.

'Remember, boy, when you so casually wander off into your dreams, we are left here alone, lonely in the cold night. Do you know what terror bequeaths the darkness of a lonely dreamless mind?'

Aryan did not know how to respond. He did not understand why he was responsible for all around him. Since he had awoken, he had begun to be rather frivolous with his thinking. The words of his company made him feel guilty. He did not know if this was right. Must he bear a burden for the need of voices around him? It seemed currently that he did not have much choice anyway.

'Poetry of the mind,

Chaos,

Are you blind?

Before you search for what lies beyond,

Look here, for here we rest, bone dirt and all.'

Aryan heard these words resonate through his mind. Is this truly the end and beginning? Would not his journey continue when his eyes shut? Questions plagued his mind, and he knew it was for all to hear.

'What point is it to dream of unfathomable memories when you will return here to the comfort of our words?'

'What makes you think your words are comforting, Mr Mikhail?'

'There is a rebel in your thought. These are not your words but of another. Remember, boy, the sea is clear, yet you cannot see the bottom, for darkness cloaks the clearest of clarity.'

There was total silence. Then the thoughts started again. Aryan always believed his thoughts were his own; this was difficult to perceive. He had forgotten to blink. As he lay on the floor, pain was flooding his body; he felt the taste of iron in his mouth. He was fading away; his vision slowly faded. In the background, he heard the voice of Lokhvitsky.

'In the event of an aerial battle between a housefly and a wasp, who would win? On first glance, it would be the wasp, but when you dwell upon it, the housefly is quite deceiving. I really cannot say.'

17

HER

Aryan stood leaning against his kitchen counter. It was made of black granite, its surface cold and hard. It was a hot day, and any cold was welcome.

He was waiting for the kettle to whistle so he could have some coffee. Outside the kitchen window, he could see the cobbled path leading to his door, and beyond that, a few flowerpots with dried leaves and a rather under-maintained wrought-iron gate. It was rusting, one side was unhinged and off the pivot.

He avoided noticing such miscreants of the mind; however, today he was rather twitchy and nervous. It was almost noon, and the room Mila slept in was closed. He hadn't got much sleep, or at least that is what he imagined, for his eyes were lazy and his body heavy.

He had dreamt of dragons and death and of losing Mila. He didn't remember his dreams usually, yet this morning he did, his chest still throbbed from being pierced by a steely knife in his dream. Maybe that was reality.

A drop of sweat trickled down his brow and fell on the kitchen floor. It was stained with years of use and lack of cleaning. It gave the entire space a rather chaotic appearance, yet it felt warm, almost like home.

The kettle whistled his coffee was ready. For once, he couldn't care less about his smouldering, hot beverage.

It was to be his third cup since morning. He was almost satiated; luckily, his love for coffee was strong, for it gave him company in restless moments like these. He couldn't recall when he was this anxious last. It evaded his mind, maybe never. This was a strange emotion to him, something he had a lack of experience dealing with. He couldn't understand how to deal with it.

His lack of companionship made it harder, for he knew not how it was to react appropriately in a situation like this.

'I ought to get me some new friends. Maybe I can sketch some out and ask them how they feel about such a scenario.'

He giggled to himself and then took a sip of coffee. It was a nervous giggle, for even though he was sarcastic, his mind seemed to consider it quite seriously. Aryan walked out of the kitchen; his back was arched slightly.

He couldn't recall if he had eaten anything, but he didn't feel very hungry. He seated himself on the dining table in the living room. He hadn't used it in an exceedingly long period of time. The dark wood was covered in a layer of dust. A lonely paper lay in the corner; it had a half-full cup of something in it, probably old coffee from the last time he sat there.

The paper and the cup were both covered in a layer of thick dust. He could see her door as he sipped on his coffee. He was resting his elbow on the dusty table, legs crossed, trying to behave casual.

Any onlooker would agree with much gusto that it wasn't working. Aryan got up from his chair and picked up the paper, dusting it. It was the last time he wrote.

'An enigma glanced by me,
Shadows danced upon us.
The sun and the moon,
They played games.
They hid and ran.
The sky only wept.
Creaking swings in barren parks,
Only echoes now laughter and all.
The breeze carried memories.
What was lost will be found,
For none is lost till truly found.'
'That was lovely.'

Aryan looked up, and there she was.

'I didn't mean to read that out aloud.'

'I'm glad you did.'

She gave him a gentle smile.

'Come, let's go!'

Aryan looked surprised. He did not anticipate going anywhere.

He was wondering if he had missed something from the conversation they had the previous evening, for he had spent most of his time looking at her.

He was certain he couldn't have missed her words; he wouldn't let his mind make a folly like that, not with Mila. He put the paper back on the table and looked at her. Her pale face was glowing, and it was accompanied by a radiant smile.

'In one of my restless nights, I created a character. He had an alter ego who stood next to him, identical yet absolutely different. They were clowns, messengers of my dream. Then one day when I awoke I forgot about them. I never felt them again, nor did I hear them. Maybe I abandoned them. They were still incomplete. Sometimes when I think of them, I wonder where they went. I feel sorrow, for I created and abandoned. Now they tread in lost dreams somewhere alone and lost. The mind is powerful, Aryan. You do not realize the lives you alter with your thought. The lost clowns, maybe you will meet them someday.'

Aryan sat down. He had met them before, and he remembered their message. They had been visitors of his thought—real or illusion, he did not know. Their words eluded him, for his mind was convoluted with thoughts of Mila. He knew she would go; he knew she was going.

'Don't look so lost, Aryan.'

She gently held his wrist and pulled him towards her.

'I saw two bicycles outside. Are they yours?'

'Yes . . .'

'Well, the day is too beautiful to spend brooding indoors.'

Aryan's mind had already accepted; the warmth of her hand had frozen him. Her face was so close to his, he couldn't think. She laughed and pulled him closer to her. Putting her soft lips close to his ear, she whispered, 'It's okay, come now.'

Aryan followed her. She was wearing a short black dress, with her back visible. It was held up by short sleeves. Her back was slightly freckled from being exposed to the sun. To him her imperfections were perfect. It made him believe she was real, yet his mind felt deceived. Her hair fell just below her neck, ruffled and untidy. She was wearing the same Oxfords from earlier, their heels enhancing her pale legs. She was carrying her tan-brown bag slung across one shoulder. In the light of the day, he could see that it had been worn out with use.

Aryan's heart was pounding again, all he wanted was to hold her and tell her how much he loved her. Standing against the open door, Mila turned her head around with an antagonizing smile.

'You haven't moved.'

Aryan followed obediently. Aryan hesitated and started towards the door. He wondered if she could feel his gaze constantly focused upon her. He didn't want her to feel awkward, but he really couldn't help himself. They got out on the dusty porch, where the cycles lay parked against the parapet wall.

Mila skipped across and picked up a green hose meant for watering the plants and turned the tap on. The water hesitated initially and then began to flow. She giggled and sprayed the dust-covered cycles with water. She gave him a mischievous glance and turned the hose towards him.

'You seem to be covered in some dust yourself.'

A spurt of water flew at Aryan; he stood and smiled.

'You should smile more.'

His clothes were drenched, but he seemed not to have noticed. They mounted the cycles and exited the porch.

'Where should we go now? Let's be adventurous.'

Aryan followed her, letting her lead him to whatever destiny she chose apt. He was a little annoyed with his mind for making everything so poetic.

Mila was standing as she pedalled; even in effort she looked at ease. There were tall green tress all around, and a gentle breeze caressed his face. He felt calm, unlike he had ever felt before.

Aryan looked up into the skies, which had darkened; clouds covered the sun, and only a few rays of light trickled through. It began to drizzle slowly; tiny drops of cold rain fell from the skies. The sparkling drops made her hair look like a starry night sky.

She turned around, almost as if she could hear his thoughts. Aryan's hair fell over his eyes. He smiled back, and for once, it wasn't awkward. He caught up to her, and as the road led on, tiny pathways led into the moist green forest.

They turned almost in unison, letting the lost pathways lead them into a silent dream. They cycled—Mila in front, Aryan behind. She was slowing down, looking around, thinking thoughts he wished he could hear yet without knowing he knew.

A tiny brook meandered across their path; there was no road any more, just the mud they were treading on and trees holding hands. They got off their cycles and dropped them near a tree.

'Let's walk.'

|Aryan walked up next to her, and without a glance, they drifted deeper into the forest. Their feet left footprints in the mud behind them, a trail of what had passed. The leaves around them were glistening, and the fragrance in the air was haunting.

'Do you believe in an alternative existence?'

'I have never thought about it.'

'Sometimes I create characters in my mind, and I truly believe that they exist in another perspective. It frightens me sometimes to think that maybe the faces I meet and the lives that intersect with mine are my own manifestations.'

Aryan looked towards Mila. She held his hand. She walked slightly ahead of him, leading the way. Even in the cold of the drizzling rain, her hands had warmth.

'Do you believe this to be real?'

She seemed to be looking beyond what lay ahead of them, not glancing even once at Aryan. It seemed to him like he was just an insignificant moment in her thought. She was contemplating deeper realities of the cold night to come; he was only an interlude in a passing monotony.

'Does it matter?'

He had never considered the concept of illusion and reality; it was dreary to his already dreary mind. This rainy afternoon, though, as he walked beside his pale companion, the thought of being an illusion to her frightened him.

'Illusions can be discarded with ease. Unlike reality, you can ignore the consequences of abandonment.'

Mila laughed; she seemed to have read his mind.

'Don't worry. I do not discard my illusions so easily. Our words are too strong, our thoughts too chaotic for this beautiful moment.'

Mila took her shoes off and held them in her hand. She seemed one with day and night. It was comforting to look at her, yet he knew she would go, an anxiety he couldn't help from lurking within his hollow mind.

The grass was growing wild now, and the mud below their feet was moist. As they walked further ahead, the trees opened up into a tiny circular patch of earth. The sun fell upon the clearing with grace, a lonely spot of yellow in the density of green.

She sat against the bark of a tree, her feet crossed, her arms dangling lose against her sides, resting in the mud. She was looking into the sky with her eyes shut as the bright sun illuminated her pale skin.

Aryan went and sat next to her. He had his legs crossed and his back arched. His arms rested on his lap. He did not know how to make himself comfortable next to her.

'Come here.'

Mila was smiling as she gently tapped the ground beside her. Aryan moved towards her and rested his back against the tree she lay against, her arm against his. The fragrance of her hair was intoxicating. It had the smell of summer, blossom flowers; it emanated a musky smell of wood and pine leaves.

'Aryan, tell me something, anything.'

Her voice didn't seem as it always did. Instead of the air of gaiety, it now had genuine empathy in it. She rested her head on his bony shoulder and put her arm on his.

'I can hear you breathe.'

His words came slow and almost silent. His mind was at ease. This was a moment he would never let slip from thought, yet it would be over.

The skies were empty, yet the trees watched them intently. The skies were lonely, still they stirred with magic. The breeze was cold yet laden with warmth.

'Are you a dream? If I awake, I need to remember.'

She lifted her head from his shoulder and turned her face to his. He was looking into her eyes. They were blue like a clear summer sky, yet he saw rain. Her lips touched his; her warmth was his, momentarily and for infinity.

Her breath ceased his as they lay in the grass, grasped in each other's warmth. He felt her hair as he ran his hands through them, her soft skin caressing his. He did not know how much time passed as he lay with her in the grass, but it did not matter. He would never wake to a calmer reality again. She lay beside him, her head nestled between his arms. He was alone, he knew it.

In each other's arms, they fell asleep, a dreamless slumber, for reality itself was a dream that night. When their eyes opened, the stars were shining above them. Aryan looked at her and smiled. She did not smile back. Her eyes were lost. Their blue showed lament. He knew he was alone now.

18

The Illusionist

Urien stood tall. His face was distorted, coloured, a smile convulsing through dark eyes.

'Darkness does not spread chaos,

Smiles do.

Dreams do not carve destiny,

For there are no dreams.

Look at you, boy,

On your knees,

Philosopher of irony.

I waited for you,

We all did.

You never came, you fool.'

Aryan was trembling. He was looking up at Urien. He was on the same path where he began his journey. The trees had dried; there was no breeze, only haunting negativity of lost beliefs.

'When the jester rode through the night, we stood and watched.

When the moon went red, we stared and wept.

When light was dreaded, and flaming embers trembled, we waited.

You never came.

You only heard her voice and left us all to fade.

Do you know who you are?'

'I . . .'

There was a flash of thunder, and day turned to night.

'Don't muster the courage to speak to me.

You voice is trembling,

It must.

You are a lie, I am not.

You are the illusion I am not.'

Aryan was looking at Urien; his feet were of the ground, his face gleaming with hate. There was no emotion in his charcoal-black eyes, he was burnt from within.

'The darkness has taken me.

You see it now, do you not?

For I can hear you yet,

Clear like a drop of water.'

His hair was flowing in the darkness; his once regal and princely robes were tattered and ravaged, yet he looked anything but diminutive, far from it.

'I did not intend for any of this. I do not even know what I have done.'

'You are not master any more,

Your mind is not yours,

A single voice,

A single smile,

And you let it all go.'

Urien's smile had vanished. He stood hunched. It seemed almost as though all the burden of lost dreams had been set upon him.

'You let the prince die.

He was not yours to let go,

Without him, we are nothing but faint.'

Urien was back on his feet, his eyes staring at his feet. The sky was bright, yet it continued to rain. He was shivering, colour dripped off his face. His shoulders drooped down; he was a figure of someone who had lost it all. He had aged. His wrinkles were visible, and his body had diminished. Time had passed too much. He seemed almost to be a projection of Aryan, lost in the summer days. Aryan stood up, his back straight, his eyes cold.

'All I wanted was for her to love me.'

'Love, how can she love you when you yourself doubt your mind?'

Urien looked up; his distorted smile was still upon his face. It was full of dread. He walked towards Aryan, leaving behind a trail of red. He was almost in touching distance.

'She held you in her arms, you accepted. Yet you do not know why?'

Aryan at this moment, standing where he was, truly believed in Urien's words. He had failed him. He remembered when he walked out of the door, anticipation upon the brows of dreams around him. He had abandoned them, left them to their own plight.

'So now you know. I am old now, I waited Aryan, and we all did. Now it is late. The sun is fading.'

Urien turned his back to Aryan and walked away along the cobbled pathway. There was a mist, and he disappeared into it. Aryan looked around him; all had changed. Trees had dried; leaves had passed. Moss grew between the cobbled pathways beneath his feet.

Aryan knew many nights had passed since he was last here. The path to his light had been abandoned; time had not waited, not even in illusion. The once-mighty Urien had aged, his hair had gone grey, and his strength for truth had passed. Yet only one thought plagued his mind. Where was she?

Aryan had to know; he began walking along the cobbled pathway, the meandering cobbled pathway upon which once rested his desires and anticipation, only in this moment there was none. He was the lonely jester. Now he knew what Urien meant. He had let the night envelop his thoughts, and as he lay on the white mattress, avoiding dream and illusion, reality had passed; time had drifted. What once was now wasn't.

'There is no light ahead,
You left it behind.
And there is no darkness either,
You swallowed it.
Now you walk in void.
What lies between day and night,
In limbo was my mind.
And in loss was yours.
Be not afraid,
For passing is a must.
Dread not your fate,

For now it is sealed.
Once the sparrows graced the seas,
Once the ravens felt the breeze,
Stagnant and still,
Poised.'

Urien had passed. Were his dreams truly dying? Were the faces and voices truly passing? A cold shiver ran down his spine. What worried him was not the fact that Urien was lost, for he would never be lost, his voice still resonated in his clarity. The mist was growing dense; he saw shadows walking towards him.

Aryan did not know how to respond, so he stood waiting. He did not hope or anticipate. If this was to be the end, he was willing to accept it for slumber in universal darkness is better than treading through misty cobbled pathways full of carcasses of thought. As the figures walked through the mist, he saw their definition. They were identical. They were the lost clowns.

'We have met before, have we not?'

Their eyes were burning red, their face grey; he could see patches of morphed brown skin behind the paint. They were humming a tune. As they spoke, he saw their teeth, sharp like razors.

They didn't seem to notice him. They walked right by, not uttering a word to him. He remembered them from an earlier thought. They were the bearers of the letter. They were happy then, their smiles real. Maybe the mist was deceiving their true appearance?

Aryan felt hesitant, for never before had he been able to recall thoughts. Now visions of the past were flashing by his empty eyes, reminding him of what has been. He had always wanted memory, but this was not warm. This frightened him, for memory was appearing yet it seemed too late. Had all thoughts morphed and merged into a singular mass of negativity?

Aryan looked ahead of him. There was only mist, and he did not have the courage to tread through the lost paths. He turned around. The wind was howling. He could hear sorrow; he could feel it within.

He walked back from where he came. Maybe the journey was over, and maybe it was time to return. Aryan treaded the cobbled stones; his bare feet felt the cold of the ground below. It wasn't the only cold he felt. Shivers ran down his spine. He was abandoning all, and in this moment, he felt it. He had turned his back to all he believed in.

Love was just a symphony meant to pass. Dreams would come; dreams would go. Only the bitter aftertaste remained. He was not the man he once believed himself to be. Celestial gods in the sky had betrayed his faith.

'In empty darkness, we walk,
Magic lost, magic found,
Within my dreary ego,
I saw candlelit dreams,
Perspiring in the hollow skies,
My thoughts were truly lost,
And then the clouds parted,
I thought I would see light again,
Betrayed by this thought,
Meandering illusions,
Of fate and random chaos,
I turned my back against the light,
I felt the darkness close and bright,
In the faith of the lonely eyes,
I am only and only seeker,
Or destiny has passed me by,
All I see is fate lost in memory,
Believe me,
For I am just a boy,
The illusionist.'

The melody filled his empty mind. When would he see her again? Her smile enticed him even now; she haunted him, crept upon his fragmented thoughts, glue to lost ideas.

A door, the door lay ahead of him. It was the same door he had longed to pass, yet now there he was, looking at it from the other side to open and return. There was no gleaming light upon it. It carried no temptation, and this was home to him, was it not?

He was just a carcass waiting to lie down. All was lost before he could even find. He pushed the door open. There was no anticipation, only agonizing loss. His heartbeat was slow, almost insignificant.

There was momentary darkness. He felt almost glad, the lost prince. He would never sleep on the cold floor again, for what dreams remained was convoluted with pain. He wished never to wake up again, just to hold her hand.

The room brightened, he wasn't home. He was almost glad. He was in Mila's room, the room she had abandoned. A lonely canvas lay resting against the window, no colour, no thought.

Parchments of paper lay scattered across the floor. He dared not look into her dreams, for he might dream again. He looked up, and across the cold floor stood the two clowns talking to the night. Their teeth gleamed in the yellow light, their face smudged with an everlasting agony. He had walked into her lost thoughts.

'She never lost them, she only abandoned them.'

'She never lost them, she only abandoned them.'

Their disjointed voices echoed eerily in the dimly lit room. Aryan looked at the parchments. They were blank, for her thoughts were alive, awakened by his presence. Had he treaded into her vision?

'You never left, she did.'

'She never left, you did.'

They were standing in a darkened corner of the room yet were illuminated by an eerie light.

'There are more of us.'

'There are more of us.'

It was dawning upon him the wasteful nature of human thought. It frightened him to believe how thoughts created in a mind truly existed.

'Like us, you to have been abandoned, just a forgotten thought.'

'Like us, you to have been abandoned, just a forgotten thought.'

The parchments of paper lying around their feet were swirling now, rising from the dusty floor, almost enticing him.

'Come, be one with ink and paper, join our story.'

'Come, be one with ink and paper, join our story.'

He loved her. Becoming one with her dream tempted his fate. What if she remembered and returned? Should he join them and wait.

'This is your fate, do not hesitate.'

'This is your fate, do not hesitate.'

129

Their eyes were gleaming, and they seemed without moving to gain on him. Aryan's mind was being morphed by their words. Their smiles gleamed cruelly in the light. Shadows beneath their eyes made them look like they were burning.

They were tempting him into an unknown darkness.

'I shall not.'

Their eyes seemed full of rage. They grew taller; the light was flickering around them. Their voice became one; it was thin and desperate yet frightening.

'You dare disobey us.'

Aryan was staring at them; he couldn't feel his legs any more.

'We are yours, and you are ours now. This is your doing.'

A cloud of darkness spread over them. He could only see their gleaming red eyes as they towered over him. Their fiery gaze was creating ripples in his conscience. He could see him being sucked into their beings. As he stood, he saw himself step out and walk towards them. He was translucent. Aryan stood still. He wasn't afraid any more. His conscience entered into his again. He felt strength. The overpowering clowns diminished in size; their faces betrayed surprise.

'Gone are the days when you cheated me. I have knowledge, you cannot fool me, I know who you are, and you cannot destroy me.'

19

The Awakening

'Everything that is conditioned is impermanent and transient.'

Urien's voice haunted Aryan. His eyes remained shut; he couldn't open them. He lay on something soft and comforting; he knew the voice wasn't a dream. Urien had gone, but fragments of his words still wandered the universe.

'There once lived a little girl. She had eyes like the sky, and her voice tinkled like silver. In the bright of the sun, she would dream of night. When night came, she would lie on her back and stare into the darkness with her gleaming jewels high above in the sky.

'She had but one dream, and that was to be able to fly. She wanted to touch the stars, for a boy once told her there were great men of the past looking down upon her, not celestial gods watching upon us. The boy said he would return, but with these words, he never did.

'She wanted to meet these men and thank them, for they kept her warm at night. The sparkle kept her safe. She never dreamt of walking through the woods. She never dreamt of swimming far out into the sea. She never dreamt of calming gods and praying on her knees. All she wanted was to fly. The boy never spoke to her again, and as her father read her a fairy tale with knights and monsters, all she wanted was to be able to fly. All night, she would look high above out of her tiny window. All night she would see the stars twinkling magical and bright, conversations in the night, one star to another, but never to her.

'She would hope and pray that one night a star would descend and show her the true warmth of the night. She hoped one night she would sprout wings and fly up to them and smile.

'She was pale in the moonlight. He watched her sleep. Her dark hair was long, dark, and tangled. She was just a child, yet her face was aged with thoughts and dreams.

'Summer passed, and so did spring. She shivered in the winter night, yet his voice never came. Why she waited, she did not know, for what are prophecies? She was just a child.

'Then one night as she lay in bed, not once losing faith, she heard his voice. "Stand up, little one, it's time to fly." She stood on the sill and sprouted wings. His voice kept her still. She flew towards the sky. She flew towards the stars, not once looking back. The night is bright. The breeze is light. Tonight we fly, stars and all.

'She looked below. The city gleamed. She never knew she lived in the stars. High in the sky, she looked down again. "This is strange, I thought the stars were above."

'She flew and flew. Sparkling bright in front of her, she saw the night. "Welcome, child, now you know what lies above lies below. All is myth, all is dream. Go back home." The night fades. A tear sparkled in her eye. The boy spoke, "Do not heed, his voice untrue. Lament in dream, smile in dream. Now we return, for the stars cease to shine." He held her hand. She couldn't see him, yet as she lay back down, all she knew was she would wait for him.'

There was a pause. It seemed almost as though Urien's fragmented voice was waiting for him to realize. Aryan knew, yet he could not understand.

'See the dry leaves,
Lying on the pathways.
See them yellow,
Their veins sooty black,
Isolated from their companions,
Scattered and decaying.
Some day you to will be separated from the skies,
One day you too will pass,
Your dreams,

These voices,
We all are leaves,
One day you will realize where we fell from.
Not the heavens,
Not the gleaming midnight sky.
We are not meteorites,
We are far less significant,
As you lie, time has passed,
As you dream, leaves have fallen,
It might be too late,
Yet she waits.
Yet she dreams.
Like you, one last smile,
Like you, one last memory.
When will you return?
When will you hold her?
Feel her breath,
Embrace her warmth.
You have been afraid too long,
You have been silent.
We have faded,
We are memory,
Will she be one too?
Haunting dreams,
Of lonely love,
Think of her one more time,
Don't you miss her voice?'

Aryan knew he spoke of Mila, yet his eyes remained close in dread and dream. Where would he be when he opened them, in darkness or light?

'Goodbye, Aryan, I have passed, and so has my voice. Now it is your dream and yours alone. Smile, for you yet can. I'm sorry, Aryan.'

Aryan felt the warmth of a hand stroke his brow. It lingered momentarily, and then it was gone. His eyes opened; he began to weep. How much time had passed, he couldn't tell. He dare not look at a reflection. Aryan got out of bed; he knew she had left.

He could sense it. He put his feet on the wooden floor. It creaked. All sound seemed magnified, and all time seemed diminished. He walked towards his door, a throbbing pain in his heart. The chill in the air made him breathe heavy; his slow stride led him to her door. It was closed but only partially. Aryan didn't knock; his hand rested on the cold steel knob.

He pushed the door open; she was gone. He walked up to her window; parchments of paper lay scattered on the floor.

'When you held me,

When you felt me,

My thoughts dreamt of you and no one else,

I yearned for a smile,

I craved for a kiss,

I got it all,

Then the yearning passed,

The day faded into night.

Smile, for one day maybe,

We will share each other's voice.'

Aryan arched his head towards the floor beneath; dried paint smudged the light-grey tiles. All around lay parchments, they were full of words; she had abandoned all thoughts.

He was afraid to read the words on the paper might he revive a lost dream. A single tear glistened in the light passing through the foggy window as it fell to the floor, dissipating and disappearing. He knew she would leave. He always knew.

He would find her, meet her one last time. He realized as he looked down that most parchments were blank. It seemed like they were now part of his conscience. He wondered why she had scribbled her last words on glass; he wondered why she had written anything at all. He was to seek her, and then she would be gone again.

Was she truly waiting? The negativity haunted his thoughts; he could not abandon this story like he had all other. Aryan knew where he would find her, if only momentarily.

'One last glance,

One last sigh,

As I walk away,

As you walk away,
Why were our destinies not meant to be?
Why this suffering?
Why this angst?
Always running,
Are we fading?'

Aryan knew where he had to go. Only this time, he would not wait for dream to lead him on. He would make the journey; this was the beginning of the end.

He would go to her. He knew he was lost, yet in this moment, he was certain. Sometimes dreams have a way of reviving sorrow. Sometimes life has a way of passing you by. Dreams had revived his sorrow, and life had passed him by, but he was craving for her smile, one last goodbye.

20

The Inverted City

The ball was over, and the jester had vanished. The puppets in the air hung limp. All had passed; all had faded.

'It's time for a story. Look beyond the clouds, therein lies your destiny. There it will end, and there it shall begin. Someday you will know of what I speak.'

Urien's words were resonating in his mind. They collided against the dimensions, being the one and only thought. His words were haunting him. Ahead into the infinite distance, he saw the clouds. They were misty light-grey teary.

They hovered high above where he stood, caressing the sky, enticing him to join them. He would reach them. There was no other dream. The hall around him had disappeared; he was back on the cobbled road.

His journey was at end. The trees had a certain viscosity to them. They seemed almost as if to dissolve into the cold air that was so lucky to be graced by their presence.

A mist covered their tops, dense grey mist, through which sunlight trickled sparse and varied. In the distance, the clouds were shifting shape, and dreams were taking form. The trees were tall, thin, and straight. They graced their way into the celestial skies above. The trickle of sunlight hid behind their backs, a fearful companion in dark days. The air carried with her haunting voices of once brighter memories, just lonely wordless voices.

A great sea passed in the distance; a layer of murk haunted her face as if to hide secrets from eyes, curious eyes. The waters remained still, as if waiting for some great prophecies to unveil them upon her. She seemed almost as to be holding her breath. A single bird dared to skim the surface of the eerie waters, her feet creating tiny ripples in an icy silence. Even she dared not stay long might she rudely awaken the sombre waters.

There was no depth; it appeared as though the waters went to the ends of the universe. There was no coast on the other end, nor was there a smile, just a blue sea into infinity.

He seemed to be moving fast. He could not feel his body. Only his eyes saw and his mind felt. The sea passed him by, and so had the bird. Her secrets are safe for now, just her and the gloomy waters. Looking up, he saw the clouds dissipate, yet a single grey cloud remained, motionless and brave, daring to threaten the newly found brightness with his lonely gloom. His visions awakened the voice in his head. All around was calm; all around it was sincere.

'Even the skies have sorrow,
For all evil lies not beneath,
For all joy lies not above,
In day and night, there is no bequeath,
Forever will the sky remain,
Observer of all,
Ill and dread.'

It was a strange image, for there was no sun in the sky, yet it shone bright. Her warmth persisted. Peals of laughter echoed above, yet there were no faces. The moist air seemed out of reach, yet the leaves were stirring stringent with stories.

'The trees remain, yet their memory does not,
For they have seen too much dread.
Their shedding leaves are passing memories
Of tragedy and joy they witnessed,
Now gone like lonely an autumn.
We too are leaves,
Turning to yellow,
Waiting to glide,

Waiting to fall.'

Fragments of dreams seemed to be unwitting participants of the dread around, the gloomy, frigid dreams that haunt the majestic minds of men and their gods.

For all must dream, who knows what horror reality bares in her warm eyes, her pensive watchful eyes, smiling with the gleaming stars? If thought could absorb, it would be parched now, for there was only hollow all around, just an anticipation of greater moments. The tearless skies watched him walk, waiting dreading.

'When thoughts die, memories are born.

When magic lingers idly in cold winter skies,

Mysteries travel into graceless hearts.'

Aryan kept walking, the voice in his mind giving him company one last time maybe. He was a silent observer in this hollow paradigm beyond the jesters' walls. This was just a transition; he could sense it. Like most of his journey, this too would pass, but one thing was certain. He knew he would not return. A lonesome howl pierced the empty skies. It wasn't heard, only imagined.

There was a clanking of coins and a crunch of crumbs. There was a sound of wheels on a track. It appeared as though dimensions had merged, for he was on his feet yet he felt stationary and moving at an incredible speed. His thoughts were heard. There was agony, yet no tears fell. The skies had no pity for him on this bright day. They had wept enough now they had abandoned him to his own fate.

'The sky and the earth will always share your fate,

The breeze will always caress your sorrow,

This, dear friend, is no reality,

Nor is it a dream.

You are moving from one realm to another.

Nothing is in reach and all watch,

Tremors in the abyss.'

As he moved forward, he saw a single side table and a chair next to it. It was a familiar chair; it was the chair from his room. A king sat on it; he wore a yellow-and-grey robe and sipped on his coffee. His great big eyebrows arched towards his stubby blunt nose. His eyes were cold and dark, like sight without vision. His skin was ashen, and he had three distinctive lines on his forehead, probably from frowning too much.

Not once did he glance at him; his back was hunched, and his chin rested on the palm of his hand. He was contemplating some great tragedy. He felt footsteps next to his. A girl walked next to him now. He had no idea where she had appeared from. She was gazing intently into a thick book, her feet in sync with his. He could look through her, see the trees beyond.

He couldn't see her face or her eyes. He couldn't read the words she read or hear the breath she breathed. The sky beyond the clouds enticed him into their dreamy stories of age-old tales. He dared not gaze might they see his loneliness. She had gone now. He wondered who she was.

'In necessity lies folly,

Deceiver of hope,

Master of the mind.

Thin silvery voices,

Entice you,

Lonely words tempt you,

Now you will walk,

Do not look back,

For might you fade.'

A big grey wolf stood in front of him. He stood on his hind legs and bore his fangs to Aryan. His eyes were gleaming, yet he felt harmless. He closed his mouth and whimpered slightly, then turned his back to him and walked away still on his hind legs.

There was soft laughter and rustle of paper. The scenario had changed. All had gone dark, and images were flashing past him at an unreal pace. They would not slow down. The big grey disappeared; maybe he was just out for a stroll.

'This is how it feels,

To not be able to dwell upon dreams.

When you dreams abandon you,

You are nothing but a dreamless night.'

The voice in his voice spoke of darkness and epoch. There was neither sarcasm nor emotion. It seemed like the end. A child giggled behind him. He couldn't look back. Vintage structures passed him by, abandoned and ageing through time, some yellow some cream, graced by large arches and colonnades at the entries, Broken windows and shuttered doors, endless days of work by long-forgotten hands. A dragon appeared in front of him; it seemed smaller than him.

He had three heads and seemed to be looking for something. As Aryan passed him by, he put his head under a wooden table which appeared beside him, whimpering. Aryan kept walking; no dragon in the universe would stand in his way. He could see his destiny. He had reached the end of his path; barren trees surrounded him, dry and lifeless. They were twisted and arched like tormented dreams of lost kings and dragons of the days before darkness.

Aryan looked up into the sky, and as he blinked, his world turned upside down. He stood in the clouds; they were dark and grey. The trees below were inverted; in front of him was a door. He stood and waited as the door opened slowly. His eyes gleamed, for he saw her. It was Mila.

'Welcome to the inverted city of dreams.

You remember us, don't you?

You remember me, don't you?

All stories are tragic.'

She stepped out, nimble on her feet. She wore her blue sundress, her skin pale as a twilight sky. She gleamed in the grey around her; her sun-kissed skin was bronze like the sandy beaches he dreamt of with her. Her hair wasn't short any more; straight and dark, it flowed in a windless sky. She haunted his vision. Her smile still graced her face, only this time it was powdered with sorrow and desire.

He walked up to her. She smiled at him and held his hand; he followed her through the door. It was dark; as his eyes adjusted, he realized where he was.

'This is where I began.'

'And this is where I end.'

Aryan stood in the same room where he had awoken first; he recognized his white mattress and the white side tables. He saw the radio and the clock in the dark extremities of his room. How was this possible? He had travelled far. He felt claustrophobic. Aryan walked up to her. He held her in his arms and kissed her on her red lips. She held him, her warm body cloaking his fears. She had mist in her eyes as she pushed him away.

'I waited, Aryan, time has passed now.'

As he looked at her, she was transforming. Her hair was silvery grey, and her eyes tired with passing of time. Her sky-blue eyes spoke of agony and wait.

'I've come now. How can this be?'

'I never left, Aryan, I was always here.'

Memories of happy smiles, echoes of laughter, the light, cool summer breeze filled his thoughts. Yet in her eyes, he saw only sorrow.

'Agony is bitter, dreams are a lie.'

Tears filled up in her eyes. They hurt him more than the life he lived. Her every tear reminded him of what he could never have. Mila looked at him through her tearful eyes. He still held on to her.

'When summer breeze will pass you by,

When the rushing birds smile and gaze,

When sand and grey caress your feet,

Remember me.

I have always loved you,

Yet I cannot stay,

Magic will fade,

Tales will fade,

Strangers with memories

Remember me.'

Mila smiled.

'Goodbye, Aryan . . .'

Her voice echoed; her silvery voice flowed through his thoughts. He held her tight; he couldn't let her go. Aryan kissed her again. He felt the warmth of her lips, and then it was cold. His eyes were still shut.

'Will you wait for me?'

He opened his eyes; she was gone. A mirror stood in the centre of the room; he walked up to it and looked into it. His face looked familiar.

'Welcome back, Lýpi. You are master and gatekeeper now . . .'

Her voice haunted his being one last time.

'I hope the stars shine upon you, for they have abandoned me and my abode of dreams.'

Printed in the United States
By Bookmasters